When he spoke, he was dangerously quiet

"Serena," he said, "this is treacherous country in these conditions. It's a maze of channels and creekbeds all littered with rocks and tree stumps. Even in broad daylight, it would be no easy matter to get home. Now, will you take those wet clothes off, or shall I?"

"I wondered when we'd get to that," Serena muttered.

The effect of her words was unexpected.

Sean cursed and hauled her forward so that she was half-kneeling in front of him. "If you imagine I set this all up so I could take advantage of you, banish the thought," he snapped. "If you recall, I had a golden opportunity once before. So if you're just being stubborn, allow me to show you once again what little effect your schoolgirlish charms have on me."

LINDSAY ARMSTRONG married an accountant from New Zealand and settled down—if you can call it that—in Australia. A coast-to-coast camping trip later, they moved to a six-hundred-acre mixed-grain property, which they eventually abandoned to the mice and leeches and black flies. Then, after a winning career at the track with an untried trotter, purchased "mainly because he had blue eyes," they opted for a more conventional family life with their five children in Brisbane, where Lindsay now writes.

Books by Lindsay Armstrong

HARLEQUIN PRESENTS
927—AN ELUSIVE MISTRESS
951—SURRENDER MY HEART
983—STANDING ON THE OUTSIDE
1039—THE SHADOW OF MOONLIGHT
1071—RELUCTANT WIFE
1095—WHEN YOU LEAVE ME

HARLEQUIN ROMANCE
2443—SPITFIRE
2497—MY DEAR INNOCENT
2582—PERHAPS LOVE
2653—DON'T CALL IT LOVE
2785—SOME SAY LOVE
2876—THE HEART OF THE MATTER
2893—WHEN THE NIGHT GROWS COLD

Don't miss any of our special offers. Write to us at the following address for information on our newest releases.

Harlequin Reader Service
901 Fuhrmann Blvd., P.O. Box 1397, Buffalo, NY 14240
Canadian address: P.O. Box 603,
Fort Erie, Ont. L2A 5X3

LINDSAY ARMSTRONG

heat of the moment

Harlequin Books

TORONTO • NEW YORK • LONDON
AMSTERDAM • PARIS • SYDNEY • HAMBURG
STOCKHOLM • ATHENS • TOKYO • MILAN

Harlequin Presents first edition July 1989
ISBN 0-373-11183-5

Original hardcover edition published in 1988
by Mills & Boon Limited

CHAPTER ONE

IT WASN'T raining heavily—a steady drizzle rather, but enough to make the street lights and the fabulous neon lights of Surfers' Paradise reflect brilliantly in the puddles.

Serena St John shrugged uncomfortably in her long plastic raincoat, which was a bit like wearing a portable sauna in the humid, muggy conditions. She longed to tear it off and feel the rain on her skin, but that would be the height of folly although the streets appeared deserted—it was long after midnight.

She hesitated for a moment and eyed the lone taxi in the cab rank. But she shook her head resolutely and stepped off the pavement, and almost under the wheels of a motorbike which had roared to life a split second earlier and come round the corner like a bolt from the blue.

It wasn't immediately apparent to Serena that her worst problem was not that she was now sitting in the gutter, breathless and shaken as well as bruised and grazed. But when the bike rider, who had leapt off his machine, leered down at her with a wolfish grin on his face and an unmistakable gleam in his eye, she shrank away from him.

He laughed coarsely and said, 'Well now, it must be my lucky night. Fancy running into a little dolly bird like you!'

Serena grabbed her raincoat which had fallen open and glanced around wildly, but the lone taxi had apparently decided to call it a night in the absence of her fare and all that could be seen of it was its tail lights disappearing down the street. Another wild glance revealed not a soul in sight, so she tried to scramble up and fight off the bike rider's assistance at the same time, but was unsuccessful both ways. He hauled her to her feet with another unpleasant laugh and breathed beer-laden fumes all over her.

'Let me go!' she commanded in a tight little voice as his hands lingered on her.

'Who you trying to kid, sweetheart?' he sneered. 'I've seen you before—and I know the likes of you sheilas real well . . .'

'I'll scream!' she threatened, and tried to pull away with all her strength, but he only latched on to her more determinedly as she struggled desperately.

Neither of them heard the soft shush of tyres on the wet road or the restained murmur of a powerful motor idling, but when Serena managed to get an arm free and aim a blow at her assailant's head, the deed was done, although not by her—and the bike rider crumpled into the gutter.

Serena blinked, and suddenly became aware that she was bathed in light, and that a metallic blue Mercedes had pulled up beside them. She spun around, to see another man behind her, and tensed as the bike rider sat up and groaned. Then he stood up unsteadily, surveyed the scene and, with a string of foul obscenities directed at Serena, got on to his bike and roared away.

She swayed where she stood, feeling physically sick, and, still without a word, the second man picked her up and put her into the Mercedes. He got into the driver's seat, closed his door and flicked on the overhead light again. Then he said abruptly, 'Did you know him?'

Serena took her hand from her brow and stared at the man incredulously. He was over thirty, she judged, tall and with thick tawny hair and eyes that were . . . grey or green? What wasn't in doubt, though, was that there was a restrained aura of wealth and sophistication about him, and, although he wasn't precisely good-looking, an air of intelligence.

He grinned suddenly and said politely, 'Have you quite finished? I asked you a question.'

This brought Serena up with a start. 'I did not know him,' she replied tartly. 'What do you think?'

He raised his eyebrows. 'I'm not sure what to think. Do you usually go around dressed like that at two o'clock in the morning?'

She followed his gaze down to her dirty, ripped raincoat which had fallen open again, revealing her scant costume beneath it. Her long black fishnet stockings were also torn and one knee was bleeding —and suddenly it was all too much for her on top of an arduous night's work.

She dashed fiercely at the tears on her cheeks, though, and said bitterly, 'You can think what you like. You're all the same anyway, whether you come on motorbikes or in fancy cars. That doesn't mean to say . . .'

'Then, my dear,' he interrupted, and shot out a

long arm to stop her from fumbling with the door
handle, 'if that's what you believe, why do you go
around asking for it? Little girls who go around like
that are only inviting trouble, and by the time
they're . . .' he looked at her assessingly, 'seventeen,
they should know better. And if they don't want to,'
he added softly, 'then they should be prepared to
accept other people's judgement of them.'

'Will you let me out of here!' Serena demanded,
but with a slight tremor in her voice. 'I don't have to
sit and listen to *you*, and I'm eighteen!'

'Eighteen?' He laughed. 'And gorgeous even
when you're covered with grit. Anyone with a bit of
sense would lock you away for another couple of
years. Does your family realise you're hellbent on
this course of self-destruction? I take it you work at
some fancy club . . . really, there should be a law
about letting the likes of you loose.'

She caught her breath. 'All right,' she said
unsteadily but with great restraint, 'you've had your
say. You obviously feel entitled to say these things to
me, although I can't quite see why . . .'

'I did just rescue you from God knows what,' he
pointed out.

'That still . . .' Serena stopped and bit her lip.
'Thank you,' she said then in a stiff little voice, but
couldn't resist adding, 'If you would take your hand
away, I might be able to relieve you of my trouble-
some, not to mention morally and physically soiled
person!' Nor could she resist a taunting glance at
him.

But all he said, meditatively, was, 'I don't think
I've ever seen true violet eyes before.' And before

she could do anything, he set the car in motion.

Serena gasped, but he merely advised her to leave the door alone. 'You wouldn't want to end up in the gutter twice in one night, now would you?'

'But . . . but where are you taking me?' she stammered on a note of panic.

'Where do you think?' he said casually. 'Some nice private place where we can get to know each other better.' His voice deepened. 'I'm sure I'm a better proposition than our bike-rider friend. I doubt whether he had any plans to . . . recompense you for your services. Perhaps that's why you put up such a fight?' he queried ironically.

Her tongue seemed to tie itself in knots. 'Stop,' she said breathlessly at last. 'Stop this instant, do you hear me!'

'All right,' he shrugged, and nosed the car into a parking bay beside the beach. It was still raining and the dark sea before them was indistinguishable from the land. 'This is as good a place as any to get started,' he said with a mocking smile.

'I . . .' Serena swallowed several times, then made a dive for the door handle, but it refused to budge and she realised the car had a central looking device which he had obviously operated during the short drive.

'What's the matter?' he drawled as she turned on him fiercely.

'I don't want to start *anything* with you!'

'You might not have much choice.'

'Why . . . why did you bother to rescue me if you don't believe I should have a choice?'

'It's not that I believe you shouldn't have a

choice so much as that *you* don't understand you're in no position to be——' he shrugged '—choosy.'

Serena licked her lips and tried to think, but all that came to mind was how foolish she'd been not to take that taxi . . . 'Please,' she said huskily, 'just let me go.'

'Where to? Do you live near here?'

'Not far,' she said hurriedly. 'Please . . .'

'I might,' he gazed at her lazily, 'when we've sorted some things out. Are you, for example, trying to impress on me that although you're all dressed up—or should I say down—in an abbreviated bunny-girl sort of outfit designed expressly to have men ogling you, you *wear* the thing and work in a place men patronise for that purpose at the very least—are you trying to tell me you resent it when they do? Do you know what kind of girl that makes you?' he asked softly.

Serena was silent, painfully silent.

'Or perhaps you feel a prim, virtuous, outraged image adds a little spice to the proceedings. Shall we . . . test it out?' He leant towards her and put his hands on her shoulders.

Serena shrank back and tried to twist away, but her struggles were puny compared to the sheer strength of his arms and she found herself half sitting, half lying in his embrace with his grey-green glance glinting down at her.

'Don't fight me, sweetheart,' he murmured. 'You'll only get hurt.'

She refused to heed this advice, but although she didn't get hurt, she finally lay still in his arms, quite exhausted.

'That's better,' he said softly. 'And just in case you're untutored in this art, let me show you how it's done.' He lifted one hand and idly traced a line from behind her ear down the slender column of her neck to the base of her throat. It was a gentle, caressing touch and he continued, pushing her raincoat off one shoulder and exploring her bare skin, the swell of her breasts above the heart-shaped bodice, her nape beneath her hair. And all the time, he watched her from beneath half-lowered lids.

Serena thought afterwards that there must have been something hypnotic in that oddly dispassionate yet intent gaze, something that held her riveted, her lips parted, her heart hammering and her limbs paralysed.

Then he lowered his head and she felt his lips against her own, covering them, kissing her . . .

Serena had never been kissed in earnest before, had shuddered at the very thought, but now some strange lethargy seemed to have invaded her. Not that she responded, she didn't even close her eyes, but it was as if a curious awareness came to her. The feel of this man was different. And he had somehow contrived to make her feel different, smooth and soft, small and vulnerable, in need of the protection his arms offered . . .

All this was extremely bewildering, and as he lifted his head and flicked on the overhead light again, that puzzlement was mirrored in her wide, dark-lashed violet eyes before she blinked.

'That wasn't so bad, was it?' he said after a moment with a rather wry smile twisting his lips.

Serena frowned and said foolishly, 'They're

green, not grey, your eyes.'

'Be that as it may, petal,' his lips barely moved, 'you don't know a lot about kissing, do you?'

'I . . . not a lot,' she whispered.

'But you aim to learn? Perhaps you've just been waiting for the right man to come along to . . . hitch your star to.'

Serena blinked again.

'Well,' he said, 'you've stopped fighting me. Comfortable? Yes?' He didn't wait for her to reply. 'Shall we proceed, then?'

'Proceed?' Serena echoed dazedly. 'Do you mean . . . ?'

'What else?'

'I . . . oh!' She tried to wrest herself out of his arms, but he only laughed at her, and said,

'Don't kid yourself, darling. Even if you wanted to, which I have to doubt, there's no way you could prevent me from doing whatever I liked. Is there?' And he tighte ed his embrace fractionally but unmistakably.

Serena could only nod, a tiny movement of her head, too petrified to speak. And for a bemused moment, she thought she detected a slight softening of the mockery in his eyes. But what followed was even more surprising. He loosened his arms, brushed a strand of hair from her eyes and sat her upright in the corner of her seat. Then he pulled her raincoat about her as modestly as was possible.

'Let that be a lesson to you, then, kid,' he said in a suddenly completely impersonal voice. 'Just in case you haven't yet travelled too far along this road you've chosen. In fact let it be two lessons. First, there are certain positions a girl can place herself in which lay her open to exploitation, and secondly, that exploitation needn't even come in the form of brute force. There are a lot of men who know only too well how to chat up impressionable little girls, and just as well how to dump them. Life can be tough enough without exposing yourself to it like this.' He turned away from her. 'Now, where do you live? I'll take you home.' He turned the key and the engine sprang to life.

Serena tried to speak several times, but finally she could only stare at him.

He said patiently, 'You do have a home to go to, don't you?' as he reversed the car around.

She closed her mouth and cleared her throat. 'Yes,' she managed gruffly, and gave him the address.

'Do your parents live there?' he queried.

'No, I . . . live on my own.'

'Of course. And I suppose you're a poor orphan with not a soul in the world to care for you?'

Serena bit her lip at the irony in his voice.

'Is that why you've come down to this?' he continued. 'Or has some man already dumped you—it's the next left, isn't it?'

When she didn't answer, only tightened her lips, he added, 'If you think you can avenge yourself against men in general this way, that's also plain lunacy.'

Serena gasped and found her fighting spirit returning to her. 'I don't . . . it's no such . . . you obviously didn't think I *kissed* with much experience! Stop here,' she ordered. 'It's this house.'

He pulled the car up but didn't unlock the door for her. 'That might not be a matter of no experience—simply that you haven't been very well taught. So, it's farewell. I'd like to think you'll go to bed and think about what I've said, but in any event, take care, little one.' He leant across her and opened the door. 'Out you get.'

Serena tossed her head, then hesitated, wondering suddenly if she could make this man understand that she wasn't any of the things he thought she was.

But when he drawled, 'Oh no, you don't. I must tell you I prefer my ladies a little older, a little more sophisticated—and a lot cleaner. Off you go!' she jumped out of the car with but one thought in her mind, that she'd die of anger and mortification if she ever saw this man again.

This sentiment was reinforced as she heard him call softly, 'Goodnight, petal.' She ran up the path towards the old weatherboard boarding house as if pursued.

Once in the safety of her room she sank down on to the bed, then jumped up almost immediately and tore her raincoat off and hurled it into a corner. Then she removed her 'abbreviated sort of bunny-girl' costume and long black stockings, screwed them all up in a ball and sent it flying across the room to join the raincoat. She grabbed her wrapper from its hook on the door and her spongebag and marched down the passage to the bathroom, where she activated the creaky old plumbing with sublime indifference to the fact that so doing at such an ungodly hour would earn her a scolding from her landlady—she normally sponged herself down awkwardly in her basin in her room after a night's work—and finally she sank into the bath with a sigh of relief.

Half an hour later she was back in her bedroom with the door firmly locked and every square inch of her scrubbed and glowing, with the exception of her knees and elbows, and to those she applied some antiseptic. She also discovered a darkening bruise on her other arm between her shoulder and her elbow.

At last she lay back in bed and switched out the light. 'That's it,' she told herself. 'An extremely humiliating night of your life which you'll just have to forget. It's quite simple . . .'

But it proved less than simple to fall asleep, she found, and also to evict a pair of grey-green eyes from her mind. To make matters worse, when she finally fell asleep, it was to dream of jungles and a tiger with strange eyes, and herself running and stumbling through the green, leafy undergrowth convinced the beast was pursuing her remorselessly, but at each confrontation the tiger paused, glanced at her, then continued on its way.

'Can't come in tonight? Why's that?' the voice said down the telephone.

Serena juggled the receiver to a position cradled between her ear and shoulder so that she could examine her bruised arm and scraped elbow.

'Well, it's like this, Tony,' she said, still squinting awkwardly downwards, 'I . . . well, I fell down last night and I got a few scrapes and bruises. I think I'd look a bit silly if I appeared in my costume, you know.'

There was a long silence, during which time she could vividly picture her employer's reaction to her news. He'd be running a hand through his unruly locks and chewing his cigar.

'Tony?' she said tentatively.

'Uh-huh,' he replied heavily. 'You trying to tell me you ran into a two-fisted door? Like the kind that dispenses black eyes?'

'Two-fisted door?' she repeated, mystified. 'Black eyes? I haven't got a black eye . . . do you mean . . . do you think . . .?'

'Yes,' he interrupted. 'Or rather I did,' he amended. 'I mean my mind just naturally sprang to a lovers' tiff. They happen, but it never ceases to amaze me the inventions some girls come up with to explain them away. On the other hand it's also dawned on me that it's Serena I'm talking to, which means there *could* be another explanation. Why don't you hit me with the full story, kid? It might just surprise me.'

'I doubt if that's possible, Tony,' Serena said hotly into the telephone, 'but just for the record, I will.'

She did, although she glossed over her encounter with the man with the Mercedes.

His sigh, when it came down the line, was heavily audible. 'Honey,' he said finally, 'built into your salary there's an allowance that covers taking a taxi home from work. I did explain that when I hired you. Did I or did I not, Serena?' he demanded sternly.

'You did,' she said in a small voice. 'But I . . . well, it's not far and I'm trying to save, you see. I guess it was a silly thing to do, though. I promise I won't do it again,' she added with a plea in her voice.

'You're right, you won't, kid. And I'll tell you why. Now you're going to hate me for this, but believe me, I'm acting with your best interests at heart—and mine to a lesser extent. You're wrong for the job, Serena. It's as simple as that. And I'm going to hire someone else in your place today.'

'But, Tony,' she stammered, 'I know I broke all those glasses, but it only happened once. You said yourself I was improving!'

'It's not the glasses,' he replied flatly, 'although I must admit I've never seen anyone break so many in one go before—it's *you*. You're just not the right type of girl for this work. You—look, how can I put it? I'm not running a brothel here, as you very well know, but I've never denied that the waitresses are here to be looked at and admired. Now there are some girls who can handle that and they can handle the customers if they get a bit too forward, and they can do it without making a big thing of it and without me having to go into bat for them, although I'm always there just in case. You can't handle it. You get flustered if anyone so much as looks at you, and God knows, if anyone tries to lay even a friendly hand on you—well, I still have the bill for six dozen glasses on my desk—I even thought of framing it . . .'

'If they hadn't been all stacked together like that, it might not have . . .'

'That's beside the point, Serena. The other thing is, you've got *me* going around like a mother hen protecting her chick. Now that's kinda defeating the whole purpose. Do you understand that, love?'

'I . . . suppose so,' Serena said desolately.

'Good.' Tony was brisk now. 'And I'm going to tell you something else. Despite all that farradiddle you told me when I hired you, and God knows why I ever did it in the first place, I must have been desperate—but despite all that, I'm pretty sure you've got a good home waiting for you somewhere—I can tell it by the way you talk and walk and look so surprised at us lesser-educated mortals and our antics . . . Well, you go back to it, Serena. Swallow your pride and do it, kid. Believe me, it's the best thing you can do.'

Click.

Serena stared at the receiver in her hand, then slowly replaced it. So that was it. Her first attempt at independence a dismal failure. She stared in front of her for a long time, then tossed her head suddenly. You may be down, Serena, she told herself, but you're not out. It wasn't much of a job, and to be honest, I *wasn't* very good at it. Besides . . . well, I'd hate to think he was right about *anything*, Mr Mercedes, but he could have had a point . . .

She sighed suddenly and reminded herself then, though, that her resources were at a dangerously low ebb, and despite her having had an excellent education in one sense, it had not exactly fitted her for going out into the world and finding a job. She spoke fluent French but she couldn't type, she'd got a distinction in Ancient History and a credit in Geography and English but she knew nothing about computers, which ruled out hotel reception work or airlines, and to make matters worse, at eighteen going on nineteen, she was too old for all the unskilled types of jobs such as supermarket checkouts and even kitchen hands.

She brooded darkly on this for a time, the award wage system which saw employers very reluctant to employ an eighteen-year-old when they could get a fifteen-year-old and pay them less.

There was one other avenue, all the resort islands on the Barrier Reef and resorts in North Queensland, but one generally had to pay one's own fare, she'd discovered, which would leave her with virtually nothing.

To make matters worse, it was a beautiful day, it would be heavenly on the beach, which was the only thing that came free, gratis and for nothing in Surfers', but she knew she would only feel guilty about that, so she spread the newspaper despondently out on her bed and knelt on the floor as she scanned the Positions Vacant column with not much hope.

She nearly missed the advertisement as she ran her finger down the paper past Female Bar Attendants, Escorts—no shortage of employment there—and down to Typists, shorthand . . . Then her finger hovered and raced back to a longer insertion entitled Governess . . .

Her heart started to beat faster. Of course—why didn't I think of that sooner? she thought. She started to read eagerly.

Governess required to act as companion to eight-year-old twin boys on isolated grazing property. Applicants should be at least eighteen, possess a

Senior Certificate, be prepared to supervise School of the Air lessons, but, most important, be genuinely fond of children and prepared to enter whole-heartedly into their lives while at the same time exerting a restraining and all-round educational influence. Ability to ride essential. Two character references required . . .

'Yippee!' Serena jumped up and did a jig around the room. Then she grabbed the paper and recognised the name of the employment agency doing the preliminary interviews, and that pleased her further. She'd been to see them and met a friendly, sympathetic lady there. Just one problem, she thought: *two* character references? She had one from the headmistress of the famous private school she had attended, but where could she get another one from? Certainly not Tony, but maybe . . . yes, why not?

She flew out of her room and downstairs in search of her landlady, finally locating her in the laundry.

'Mrs Benson? Would you do something for me, Mrs Benson?'

A plump, middle-aged woman turned from the washing maching she was loading. 'Oh, Serena, it's you. Listen, love, I wanted to talk to you about . . .'

'I know,' Serena said contritely. 'About the bath last night. I'm sorry, but I slipped over, you see, and I was filthy.'

'Oh, well,' her landlady said grudgingly, 'so long as you don't make a habit of it. There are other people in the house and they're entitled to a good night's sleep.' She turned back to the washing machine.

'Mrs Benson,' Serena said hurriedly, 'I came to

ask you a favour.'

Mrs Benson's plump frame suddenly went still and it was a wary face she turned to Serena. 'What kind of a favour?'

'Would you . . . I mean, would you mind writing me a reference? You see, I'm applying for a governess job and I wondered if you could just say . . . that you've known me for three months now, that I don't drink or smoke, that I don't cause any disturbances—I really am sorry about the bath last night—and that I'm honest! Something like that. Would you mind?'

Mrs Benson relaxed with a laugh. 'Course I'd do that for you,' she said obligingly. 'Matter of fact, I'd be happy to. You're a good girl, Serena, and the sooner you get away from that place you're working presently, the better. I'll get my glasses and we'll do it together. You know,' she added with a smile, 'for a minute you had me worried. I thought you were going to bite me for a loan or tell me you couldn't pay the rent!'

Serena smiled back a trifle uneasily, horribly conscious that if she didn't get this job or some job soon, that would become an unpleasant reality.

They composed the reference together over a cup of tea.

'There.' Mrs Benson sat back. 'How does that sound?'

'It sounds . . . almost too good to be true,' Serena said with a chuckle. 'No men friends, no vices, a pleasant, cheerful personality. Helpful. Do you think they'll believe it?' she asked on a more sober note.

'I'll tell them the same to their faces,' Mrs Benson said tartly. 'Now if I were you, pet, I wouldn't say anything about the club. There's no need for them to know about that. Er—does the ad mention where this property is? You know, some of these western graziers can be real toffee-nosed. They might want to know about your family.' Mrs Benson was unable to suppress a note of curiosity herself, because she'd often found herself wanting to know more about this lovely, mysterious child—as she thought of Serena. Wouldn't be surprised if she came out of the top drawer herself, she'd mused. But something had gone wrong, obviously.

Serena said quietly, 'My family is my own business. After all, I'm old enough to vote now, so surely I'm old enough to be judged on myself and not my family background?'

'That's true.' Mrs Benson nodded, but a shade regretfully. 'Just thought I'd warn you. When are you going to see them?'

Serena jumped up. 'Right now. I can't thank you enough, Mrs Benson,' she said warmly, and leant over to plant a kiss on that good lady's cheek.

The next two days were extremely long.

The interview with the employment agency was hopeful, however, Serena thought. For once her age and education were in her favour, and the next morning she received a call from them asking her to attend another interview, this time with a Mrs Denby, at a luxury hotel.

'How do you do, Serena? May I call you that?'

The grey-haired motherly lady who had introduced herself as Mrs Denby smiled across the low coffee-table.

'Of course,' Serena smiled back.

'I . . . see you haven't had a job since you left school, Serena?'

'No. Um . . . I decided to take a sort of working holiday around Australia. So far it's been mostly . . . holiday. I've had a few odd jobs here and there, but only filling in.' Serena plaited her fingers in her lap and wished devoutly that she was better at lying.

'Would you be prepared to consider this job on a more permanent basis?' Mrs Denby enquired.

'Oh, yes!' Serena said eagerly. 'I mean, if I fit in . . . if you thought I was suitable, I'd be quite happy to stay.'

'What about your family?'

Serena had been dreading this question, but she managed to say equably, 'My parents are dead, although I do have a stepmother, but we're not . . . we're not very close.' She stopped and coloured faintly.

But Mrs Denby nodded understandingly. 'Tell me, have you ever lived in the country? Rosewood is fairly isolated, although we're pretty well set up, but it is a different kind of life and it could take some adjustment, especially for a city girl.'

Serena relaxed. 'That would be no problem. I was born and raised on a sheep property in Western Victoria. And I had my first pony when I was five.' She smiled across the coffee-table. 'I gather these twins are horse-mad.'

'You're not wrong there,' Mrs Denby chuckled.

'They're a sore trial to me in that respect. Perhaps I should have given you some background earlier? I'm employed as the housekeeper at Rosewood. In fact I've been there longer than I care to remember sometimes,' she said ruefully. 'Unfortunately,' her eyes saddened, 'the twins' father met with a fatal accident a few years ago, which is how they came . . . more directly into my care. And up until now it's been no problem—well, to be truthful, perhaps I should say it's been a growing problem. I'm finding it harder and harder to keep track of them and so is everyone else, which is why we thought of getting someone whose *sole* job it was to look after them. Also to help them acquire some education, otherwise there's the distinct possibility that they could grow up quite uncivilised. But their uncle, who is . . . responsible for them now, doesn't just want a teacher. He wants someone who has the time and the inclination to go riding and swimming with them, who has time to read to them and help them improve their manners. Can you visualise the kind of person we're looking for, Serena?'

'I think so. Someone to mother them a bit or to be like an older sister, perhaps.'

Mrs Denby shot her an unusually keen glance, then said smoothly, 'That's the general idea. Of course, the final decision doesn't rest with me. I'm pruning back the list the employment agency prepared to save my employer time and because whoever does get the job will be in close contact with me, so it's important we see eye to eye.'

'Of course,' Serena said quietly. 'Do . . . when do you think you'd be making a decision?'

'Possibly later today. Would you be available for another interview, say . . . early this evening?'

'Oh, yes,' Serena said fervently. 'And I have no other commitments, so I could start whenever you wanted.'

'That's good to know.' Mrs Denby rose and extended her hand. 'We'll be in touch definitely—one way or the other, my dear. Thank you for your interest.'

By six o'clock that evening, Serena was in the depths of despair, although she kept reminding herself that people's interpretation of early evening could differ. All the same, by seven she'd given up hope and was beginning to feel curiously breathless and frightened at her bleak prospects, when Mrs Benson cooeed to her up the stairs.

'Yes, I'm here,' Serena called back. 'I suppose they've chosen someone else?'

But they hadn't. Mrs Denby wanted to know if she could come back, say, in half an hour's time.

Serena put the phone down with a new kind of breathlessness. 'I might be in,' she said to Mrs Benson in a trembling voice. 'At least, I'm going to meet the boss this time. Oh dear, my knees feel quite weak!'

'What you need is a strong cuppa. I'll make it while you get dressed,' Mrs Benson said energetically. 'Off you go—don't just stand there!'

Serena smoothed her straight cream linen skirt and checked the buttons at the wrists of her matching silk blouse as the elevator bore her upwards to the tenth floor of the luxury hotel she'd visited earlier in the day. Then she touched the brown velvet ribbon that confined her abundant fair hair in a demure ponytail, and matched the suede belt at her waist and her medium-heeled leather shoes. I hope I look like a governess, she thought distractedly. At least the skirt covers my knees if I'm careful how I sit and the blouse my arms—what do governesses look like anyway? Perhaps I should have worn riding gear . . .? Oh, God, please help me get this job!

It was Mrs Denby who met her at the suite door.

'Serena,' she said warmly. 'Come in. I'm sorry we were so late in contacting you, but I decided to have a chat with your headmistress and it took a while to track her down. She gave you a glowing reference, by the way. Come right in, my dear. I'd like to introduce you to my employer, Sean Wentworth. Sean, this is Serena St John!' She moved towards an inner doorway. 'I'll leave you two together,' she said graciously, and closed the door behind her.

Serena's hand flew to her mouth as she stared across the room. And her first coherent thought was—they're *grey*, not green—about two seconds before her next set of thoughts, which embraced a sincere desire to be able to practise the ancient Aboriginal art of invisibility. But there was not a gum tree or a willi-willi in sight to aid her in this wish. Only a tall man with tawny hair and deceptive eyes, with a mocking smile growing on his lips as he drawled, 'Well, well, we meet again, petal!'

CHAPTER TWO

SERENA backed away, aware that her cheeks were flaming and her palms moist. But these were minor conditions compared to the amazing rate of her heartbeat and the sudden alarming dizziness that was assailing her—not helped by the fact that she had found it difficult to eat all day.

'You,' she said weakly, and swayed where she stood.

'Indeed,' he drawled, and frowned. 'Life is full of surprises—but you'd better sit down before you faint.'

'No . . . no . . . I think I'd better go—oh, please!' she begged as he loomed over her. But she ended up sitting in a chair while he poured her a drink and brought it over to her. 'Drink this,' he said quietly but quite determinedly.

'I . . .'

'Go on,' he ordered.

Serena twisted her hands, then accepted the glass and gulped at the fiery liquid, shuddering briefly. 'Some more,' Sean Wentworth said, and after a second gulp he removed the glass from her shaking hand and sat down opposite her.

'Well,' he said, observing the pink entering her cheeks, 'that should give you enough spirit to answer a few questions. Such as—what particular lies you

27

told Mrs Denby in order to gain this interview?'

'I didn't tell her any lies,' Serena protested feebly.

'No? That's strange,' he said evenly. 'She gave me a pretty full briefing about you, yet she never once mentioned the Pelican Club. Perhaps *you* omitted to mention it? Possibly . . . deliberately?'

The brandy hit the pit of Serena's stomach with unusual impact. 'So, what of it?' she demanded fiercely. 'You yourself told me to turn over a new leaf—only two nights ago, if you recall! But even then I got the distinct impression you were pretty free with your advice so long as it didn't involve you in any way—other than frightening the life out of me and *stealing* kisses.'

'My dear child,' he replied gravely although with a glint of amusement in her eyes, 'I'm delighted you decided to heed my advice, believe me. I'm not quite so pleased at the thought of you telling Mrs Denby a packet of lies, however. For one thing, it could have placed her in a very awkward position.'

'I didn't . . . *precisely* lie,' Serena said. 'My references are genuine and she told me she checked them.'

'And you've never heard of lying by omission?' he queried sardonically.

Serena bit her lip. Then she said tautly, 'Tell me this. How do you go about making a fresh start if you have to tell everyone you were last employed as a waitress at the Pelican Club? How many people are going to believe that I only took the job because I was desperate? Tell me that if you can.'

'Listen, Serena,' he said grimly, 'I wasn't born yesterday. There are alternatives to the Pelican Club for anyone, however desperate. There's the dole, for example. I'm sure no one would deny you social security on the strength of the fact that you could get a job in a half-baked strip joint! Then, somewhere, there's a family who obviously thought enough of you to send you to a very expensive private school which I've no doubt provided you with a top-class education and, as Mrs Denby just verified, a top class Senior Certificate, but instead, you're a thousand miles from home and trying to tell me you're destitute. It just doesn't wash, my dear. Unless . . .' He stopped and looked at her intently with suddenly narrowed eyes.

'What now?' Serena asked warily.

'Unless you're not really Serena St John at all?'

'I . . . oh!' Serena closed her mouth with a click and an even warier expression crossed her face. But Sean Wentworth was waiting, and there was an air of implacability about him that made Serena remember her dream about tigers set to pounce . . .

'I am Serena St John,' she said in a small voice devoid of inflection. 'But I realise I was wrong to . . . to try to deceive Mrs Denby like that and . . .'

'I'm glad you do realise that, Serena,' he interrupted, and stood up. She glanced up at him nervously, then down at her hands.

'Because you see,' he went on, 'and when I say this I'm not *necessarily* accusing you of it, but places of that sort sometimes have unpleasant connections with drugs, prostitution and so on.' Serena moved restlessly, but he continued, 'Again, I'm not saying that one particularly, but when you're looking for someone, to place two young children into their care, you can't be too careful about who you choose.'

'I understand,' she said gruffly. 'I wasn't involved in anything like that, and if it did go on, I didn't realise it.' She stood up herself. 'Please apologise to Mrs Denby for me. I've probably wasted a lot of her time. And yours.'

She moved around him with her fair head bent, unable to make herself meet his eyes and only too eager to get away from his forbidding presence as quickly as she could before she burst into tears at the second humiliation she'd suffered at his hands in so short a time.

It seemed he had other ideas. As she headed blindly for the door, she heard him say, 'Sit down, Serena.'

Her head jerked up and she swung round to stare at him out of huge violet eyes. He was still standing beside her chair with his hands dug into his pockets and a look of—was it amusement?—on his face.

She stood irresolute for a moment, once again curiously trapped by that grey-green gaze, and as she recalled the last time it had happened a flood of warm colour suffused her cheeks, but she shivered despite it and turned to the door again. She even had the knob in her hand when Sean Wentworth spoke without moving from where he stood.

'Don't make me have to come and get you, Serena,' he said lazily. 'You applied for this job, but I'll decide when the interview is over.'

'I . . . I don't understand,' she stammered over her shoulder. 'I thought it *was* over.'

'Not at all,' he replied blandly. 'There's a way we could . . . come to some understanding.'

Serena moistened her lips as her hand fell slackly to her side. 'What kind of an understanding?' She frowned perplexedly. 'Not two minutes ago you were accusing me of being either a prostitute or a drug addict . . . maybe *both*, or . . . or an impostor!'

'Sit down, Serena,' he said again, but this time with a decided note of warning in his voice.

She stared at him mutinously and stayed where she was. But when he came forward and forcibly propelled her towards a chair, she found her small mutiny was no match for his sheer strength.

'I thought you might have learnt something the other night,' he murmured.

'I learnt about having choices,' she flashed at him angrily as he picked up her hair ribbon and tossed it into her lap. It had come off during her undignified struggles. 'I learnt about laying myself open to exploitation, which, incidentally, was not a lesson I really needed to learn—I don't see how all that puts me in a position where I have to stand your presence a moment longer!' She glared at him.

He smiled slightly. 'You've got a lot of spirit, haven't you?' he remarked idly, then, 'Don't you *want* the job?'

Serena gasped, then started to speak, hotly and quite incoherently.

He waited until she fell silent, then said, 'No, I'm not playing any tricks on you, or teasing you—if that's what you're trying to say. All I'm doing is giving you the chance you spoke about so passionately earlier.' He leant down and removed the brown ribbon from her fingers which were fraying and shredding it with an almost demented life of their own.

'How . . . but how *can* you if you think those things?' she asked tearfully.

'Because the operative word *is* think,' he said steadily. 'I don't know—anything. Other than that, for some reason you've got yourself into a fix and I'm prepared to help you out of it.'

'But what if I am all those things?' she asked shakily. 'I mean, do you believe anything I've said or not?'

'I'm not sure what to believe. If you could be honest with me and tell me truthfully how this all came about . . .?' Their eyes clashed.

Serena hesitated, then she dropped her eyes. 'I can't,' she whispered. 'I just can't.'

'Very well,' he said after a moment with a slight shrug, and sat down opposite her. 'Then we'll have to make a bargain. If you did go off the rails for some reason, I'm giving you the chance to reform. Now,' he lifted a hand as she started to speak, 'before you get your hackles up, if that thought offends you, I'm also giving you the benefit of the doubt. For all I know you could be an innocent little girl caught up in something that wasn't of your choice. But the job is yours, provided you make these kids the most important part of your life and don't get involved in any mischief —and that includes the romantic kind.'

Serena closed her eyes and rested her head on her hand, utterly bewildered by the turn of events. How could she possibly be the victim of such a crazy coincidence, not to mention misunderstanding? If only I'd gone to the beach yesterday morning, she thought despairingly. By the time I got home they would probably have stopped interviewing applicants . . . On the other hand, was she in a position to turn down an offer of employment like this, even if it meant being put in this awful position? Of being suspect of just about every vice she could think of? Of being offered a chance to reform herself . . . She stifled the hysterical bubble of laughter that rose to her throat and took a deep breath.

'Look,' she said slowly, 'I'll take it. So long as I can make a condition.' She ignored Sean Wentworth's quizzically raised eyebrow and went on steadily, 'If I perform well, if I *reform*,' she couldn't prevent a slight twist of her lips as she uttered the word, 'and do a good job with these children, you won't ask me any more questions or probe and pry into . . . well, you know what I mean. Because if you do try to dig up my . . . background, I'll be gone so quickly you won't see which way I blew through,' she said very seriously.

Sean Wentworth regarded her enigmatically. Then he drawled, 'That might not be so easy from Rosewood, but if you want it, I'll give you that undertaking—on a limited basis. We'll make it a private agreement, renewable every month if we both wish it. But if you fall down on the job or slip off the tracks and try to deceive me about it, I'll find some way of handing you back to whoever you're running away from.'

The last was said softly but with unmistakable intent.

Serena did not miss it and bit the tip of one finger anxiously. It would be no problem to be the perfect governess, despite his doubts. The problem *was,* could she trust him to keep his side of the bargain?

She said slowly, 'It would be despicable of you to go back on your word.'

He rose and put down a hand to draw her to her

feet. 'You know the conditions—and when I make a bargain I stick to it, and you'll have to be content with that. I'm a little too old to cross my heart and hope to die.'

Serena breathed exasperatedly, feeling reduced to the age of about six. 'I don't like you very much, you know,' she said. 'You're very . . . I don't know what the word is, but it's extremely galling to be in this position, if you must know! And all because I didn't have the sense to take a taxi home one night. It's very strange how your life can . . . turn around on one small decision like that.'

'Oh, I agree,' he said gravely, his tiger's eyes resting on her half bewildered, half cross expression. 'Not to mention having the life frightened out of you and kisses stolen from you. You'll just have to put that down to my Good Samaritan instincts. Incidentally, I'd be prepared to pay you a week's salary in advance to help you with any . . . commitments you might have. Would that help to raise my reputation in your esteem any?' he queried, his eyes still roaming her face and glinting with mockery.

Serena swallowed and took refuge in honesty. 'It will help with my rent. Thank you,' she said primly.

It occurred to Serena, among a host of other perplexing and irritating thoughts, during the next few days, that Sean Wentworth had mentioned the Pelican Club by name before she had. How had he known it was that club? she wondered. There were several in that area, and nothing about her costume mentioned Pelican specifically. So he must have recognised the costume, and that meant he must have *been* there himself. Of all the hypocrites! she thought. But common sense prompted her, not that it was easy, but all the same, to banish all the ire she felt towards her new employer. No, not easy, she mused, but very necessary.

The other thing that occurred to her was that no mention had been made of the twins having a mother. Mrs Denby had said that their father had been killed, not parents but *father*. Was there a mystery about their mother? She shrugged and decided that all would be revealed to her in time, no doubt.

A week after that disastrous interview, her transformation from unsuccessful club waitress to governess came about, and it was a day that had an almost dreamlike quality to it, she thought, as she stood on the steps of the historic Rosewood homestead and watched the sun set.

She'd been flown up from Coolangatta that morning in a light aircraft that bore the legend 'Rosewood Holdings' on its white-painted exterior. She had been the only passenger and had shared the aircraft with a variety of cardboard cartons and the pilot, who had introduced himself as Bill O'Grady.

They hadn't been in the air long before Bill, a tall, spare man with a fringe of fluffy grey hair, had told her in clipped sentences of almost monosyllabic brevity that they'd be seeing a lot of each other as he too lived at the homestead along with Sean Wentworth and his nephews and Mrs Denby.

'Going to need your wits about you,' he had also remarked.

'Oh, why?'

'Greased lightning,' he'd offered.

'The twins, you mean?'

'Sure do. Nice kids, though.' He glanced at her then a little assessingly and had seemed to want to add something, but when he did speak again it was only to point out that they were over the Range and now traversing that vast, fertile area of Southern Queensland known as the Darling Downs.

'It's very pretty,' Serena had said as she had gazed down at the open, rolling countryside below, crisscrossed with its patchwork paddocks of grain and green contours.

'Yep. Not so green and pretty around Rosewood.'

'No? Tell me about Rosewood,' she had encouraged.

And surprisingly, despite his lack of verbosity, she found, when they finally landed, that Bill had given her an amazingly accurate description of the area. More arid, less fertile was this land beyond the western extremity of the Downs. The landscape had flattened out and gone were the wheat and sorghum paddocks.

'Cattle country,' he had said laconically. 'And sheep. Might look dry and dusty to you, but it's better now than I've seen it for years.'

Serena hadn't replied as the little aircraft had floated downwards. Truth to tell, she'd been unable to find the right words to express the sudden incredible feeling she had had of space, to describe the quality of light and the stark beauty of this more austere landscape.

There had been a reception committee waiting for her at the end of the runway, in the shade of an enormous shed that housed a variety of vehicles from four-wheel-drives to heavy-duty motorcycles. And on a large concreted area beside the shed, exactly on a painted cross in its middle, stood a gleaming helicopter.

She had climbed down a little uncertainly, surprised at the number of people about and the hush her presence appeared to have created. Then two identical bundles of tanned, fair-haired energy had scampered up and introduced themselves as Richard and Cameron Wentworth.

'We're twins,' one of them had informed her unnecessarily.

'I can see that,' she had answered laughingly. 'How will I ever be able to tell you apart . . .?'

She came back to the present and smiled wryly to herself. In fact Richard and Cameron might look alike, but their personalities were sufficiently different for that not to be a problem, she hoped. What was more amazing was the size of the property, from what she had gathered, and the number of people who lived and worked on it. She had been given a guided tour of the close environs including several dams and creeks that could be used for swimming, the horse paddock, and so on, and introduced to many of the employees, and decided it was rather like a small empire. She had also been subtly initiated into what was on and off limits and formed the impression that, like an empire, there was a social ladder at Rosewood with the homestead at its peak. Also, that the position of governess was a privileged one because it included living up at the big house. If only they knew, she thought once with an inward grin at the deference she was accorded.

Sean Wentworth had stayed around long enough to make sure that most of this early education benefited from his presence, and Serena, after their first glance, had tried wholeheartedly to be as normal as possible in his company. But it was with some relief that she had heard him excuse himself finally, and leave her to Mrs Denby.

'It's been some day,' she murmured to herself, 'and not yet over.' She leant a little wearily on a veranda post, having been instructed by Mrs Denby that on this, her first night, she could leave the twins to her and relax a little before dinner.

The house was old but in excellent repair and had a veranda all round it on to which each bedroom led. Serena's section, opposite her bedroom, overlooked a patch of lawn, some flower beds and a magnificent old ghost gum that stood sentinel at a side garden gate. And just as she was thinking of going inside to get ready for dinner, a flash of pink caught her eye, alighting in the gum, then the air was filled with noisy cheeps as a flock of pink and grey galahs swooped and circled, then settled in the tree.

Serena watched, entraced, but the birds didn't stay long. They rose as if at an invisible signal, wheeled once around the tree, making an enormous noise, then headed away into the gathering dusk.

She laughed softly as peace was restored, but suddenly there were tears in her eyes and on her cheeks as she was reminded of her own home and a flock of sulphur-crested cockatoos that had visited regularly. She sniffed and thought how far away it all was now, not only in miles but in every other way, and her shoulders slumped as she tried to shut out the memories of her peaceful, happy childhood, because it never helped to think back, it only made things worse . . .

She sniffed again and turned to go inside, licking the tears from her upper lip, only to bump into Sean Wentworth.

He put out a hand to steady her.

'I—I'm sorry,' stammered Serena. 'I didn't know you were there.'

'That's not surprising.' He took his hand off her arm and gestured towards the tree. 'They make quite a racket, don't they?' His grey-green eyes rested on her own and narrowed. 'Why the tears?'

Serena swallowed several times and fumbled in her pocket for a handkerchief. 'I don't know,' she said, and blew her nose. 'It was just so lovely seeing those birds, then . . .' She shrugged and blinked several times. 'There! I'm fine now.'

Sean looked down at her meditatively before he said, 'You know, it's no crime to feel a bit lost and forlorn on your first day. But if I know the twins and Mrs Denby, and Bill for that matter, before you know it, you'll be like one of the family.'

For some reason this caused Serena's eyes to fill with tears once again and caused, for other strange reasons, Sean Wentworth to grimace, push a silky strand of fair hair behind her ear, then put an arm around her and squeeze her shoulder. 'You look about twelve when you cry,' he observed. 'Which leads me to wonder,' he added almost beneath his breath, 'whether I haven't got three children on my hands now.'

This was exactly what Serena needed, as it happened. She tilted her small chin haughtily at him, but before she could say anything he released her and glanced at his watch. 'You've got about half an hour to freshen up. See you at dinner.' And he strolled away, leaving Serena biting her lip frustratedly.

Tired as she'd been, and confused, she thought ruefully as she stared up at the ceiling of her darkened bedroom, sleep was still eluding her. The old house had settled itself for the night with a variety of creaks and strange sounds as the temperature dropped. And yet here I am, wide awake, she thought, and turned over in bed.

It was a wide, comfortable bed with a well-sprung mattress, and she certainly couldn't blame her sleeplessness on it. In fact it was just one of the many comfortable features of the Rosewood homestead. Serena had gathered from her earlier tour that it had been built about a hundred years ago, a wooden house that had been added to but still was faithfully colonial with high-ceilinged rooms and the veranda all around as protection from the heat of summer, and fireplaces for the cold winter nights. But despite the touches of antiquity and the touches of opulence, like the beautiful rosewood furniture in the lounge and dining-room, and the magnificent sea of blue, velvet-like carpeting that flowed through those rooms, it managed to be a homely house and the twins had full run of it.

The twins, she thought, and chuckled softly. First impressions had confirmed Bill O'Grady's description of them—bundles of sheer energy and possibly a lot of mischief. But strangely appealing for all that.

She frowned and tensed as a light tap sounded on the French door that led from her bedroom to the veranda. As she reached out and switched on her bedside lamp, the tap came again, then the door opened and two small boys eased themselves and one large dog into the room.

'What is it? Is anything wrong?' she asked anxiously.

It was Richard who answered after making a variety of gestures which Serena correctly interpreted as a request for her to keep her voice down. 'It's Digby,' he whispered.

'Digby?' She frowned again, then ducked as the kelpie dog, probably the most vicious-looking dog she'd ever seen besides being a veritable patchwork of unlikely colours, evaded Richard's grasp and leapt on to the bed.

'Yes, miss,' Richard went on. 'It's his birthday, isn't it Cameron—well, give or take a day or two.' He waved a hand and continued without waiting for his brother's confirmation, 'And seeing as how you're supposed to be our best friend from now on, we thought you'd like to come to his party.'

'Well, I would,' Serena said a trifle breathlessly as she tried to evade the ugly mutt, not content with making himself free of her bed but also trying to lick her face most affectionately. 'I don't think I've met Digby, though. Who is he? And when's the party—by the way, you could have asked me in the morning . . .'

But the twins had succumbed to a paroxysm of laughter and the dog was moved to utter a short, sharp yelp in her left ear which was immediately smothered as Richard and Cameron dived on him.

It took some time to extricate herself from the resultant welter of arms, legs and dogs, but when she had done it finally, it was to say in a laughing whisper, 'I get you! This is Digby, isn't it?' She indicated the dog.

'You got it,' Richard whispered back obligingly. 'Want to come? We've got it all set up in our bedroom.' He favoured her with a curiously narrow glance.

Oh, I get it, thought Serena. I'm on trial, I think. But what harm could there be in a midnight feast for a favourite dog?

Several minutes later she watched in wonder as the fearsome-looking creature devoured what Richard and Cameron solemnly assured her were his most favourite foods, all secretly prepared during the day and cunningly stored under Richard's bed. Vegemite sandwiches and lumps of cheese smeared with strawberry jam went the way of a hunk of cake and a container of melted ice-cream, all devoured with relish.

'Boy,' Cameron whispered dreamily, 'did he ever enjoy that!' He flung his arms around the dog. 'Happy birthday, Diggie!'

'He's going to spend the night with us too, miss,' Richard informed Serena. 'Don't honestly see why he's not allowed in the house, but one night can't hurt.'

But here Serena chose to draw the line. 'Listen, boys,' she whispered back as she knelt on the floor between them in the glow of one small candle planted in a cherry cup cake upon which Digby now had his eye, 'and please call me Serena, otherwise I'll have to call you both Master Wentworth, but I once had a dog who loved all these kind of foods, only he had a habit, when he had too much of them, of getting sick . . . sick as a dog, in fact . . . so we're going to have to put him out. All right?'

It was Richard who considered the matter. Then he said with a sudden grin, 'You're right. Denny would crack up good and proper. Never mind, Cameron,' he said consolingly to his twin, 'we'll take him for a swim tomorrow. Cameron's a bit soft about Digby,' he added to Serena.

'So what if I am?' Cameron retorted indignantly. 'He's a good friend.'

'I'm sure,' Serena said soothingly. 'Let's get him outside now and then I'll help you to clean up here.'

They managed to get the dog outside with the minimum of noise, although on several occasions throughout the operation, Serena couldn't help wondering what she would do if she was caught—say by her employer—creeping around the house with the twins and dog in tow. But no one stirred, and finally the bedroom was tidied up and both boys back in bed.

Serena tucked them up by candlelight and said goodnight warmly, but just as she reached the door, she was struck by a sudden thought. She approached the twins' beds again. 'How did you light this candle, boys?' she asked softly.

An uneasy silence greeted her words, then Richard said offhandedly, 'Matches. I found a box.'

'Well, I think you'd better give them to me,' she whispered back seriously. 'After all, you won't need them now, will you?' She looked from one to the other with raised eyebrows.

Richard hesitated, then with a shrug stuck his hand beneath his mattress and produced the box. A squashed packet of cigarettes fell out at the same time.

The silence was complete for a long moment until Serena finally cleared her throat and retrieved the packet from the floor, her mind working furiously. Then she said gravely, 'I'll make a bargain with you two. By rights I should report this to your uncle. But if you give me your solemn promise you won't try to smoke again, I won't tell this time. Is that a pact?'

'We don't really smoke, Serena,' Cameron whispered. 'We just thought we'd have a try—you know, a couple of puffs. We only found them yesterday. Didn't we, Richie?'

Richard was silent and his eyes never left Serena's face.

'Well now, I believe you,' Serena said softly. 'I'm not so sure what your uncle would believe, though.'

'You said you wouldn't . . .'

'Only if you promise, Richard,' she said coolly. 'And you, Cameron.' She hoped that didn't come out as an afterthought, but she had already formed the impression that Richard was the instigator of most of the trouble the twins got into. Just as she was suddenly also sure that she would have quite a few battles of will with Master Richard Wentworth before she won him over.

'OK,' Richard said at last. 'We promise.'

'Do you . . . keep your promises?' queried Serena.

'Course we do!' Richard looked quite injured.

'Good. Then that's settled,' she said briskly. 'Goodnight, boys.'

It wasn't until she reached the safety of her own room that she had to laugh a little at all that had taken place. But as she settled herself in bed once more, she acknowledged that this job was going to entail some fancy footwork if she meant to do it well. Keeping a step ahead of the handful Richard and Cameron

Wentworth represented, in other words. She frowned faintly in the darkness because in truth, she realised, she had expected two normal little boys . . . Not that they aren't normal, she told herself sleepily. But not quite as . . . open and trusting as I expected. Oh, well. It just means I'll have to be on my guard, because I intend to do this job very well . . .

She fell asleep.

CHAPTER THREE

BREAKFAST and lunch were almost always informal affairs at Rosewood. This was so even when there were guests in residence, and it was not uncommon for the permanent residents to see little of each other during the day until the evening meal. Bill O'Grady, who was Sean's right-hand man and a man of many parts as well as being residential pilot, and Sean were often up and gone before dawn and not back until dusk. This suited Serena, although she was a little surprised that she should have such a free hand with the twins right from the word go. It was during an evening meal, about three weeks after she had started, that she discovered this was not quite so, and also had her wariness regarding the twins, in a sense, crystallised.

Each evening the long, beautifully polished rosewood table in the dining-room was set, even if there were only the six of them in the house, and everyone was expected to spruce up and take their places at the appointed hour.

The twins were not much in favour of the sprucing up aspect, but Serena always changed into a frock. This night it was a pretty white voile cotton with tiny navy blue dots, no sleeves and a navy blue narrow suede belt. Flat navy blue shoes went with the dress. She brushed her hair until it was like a cloud of glimmering fairness, drew the sides into a knot at the back of her head and pinned them there, and then, on an impulse, stepped into the garden and found a sprig of white jasmine to pin there as well.

She then went to check her charges and sent Richard back to wash his ears—something that he did so scantily that she sent him back again.

The result of this was a Richard muttering darkly beneath his breath as he finally took his place at the table.

'What was that you said, Richard?' Sean enquired as Mrs Denby served her delicious homemade soup.

'I said,' Richard retorted clearly, 'that Sammy Banks doesn't have to scrub his ears before he's allowed to eat his dinner, so why should I?' He cast Serena a cross look.

Sammy Banks was the son of one of the boundary riders. He had lost his mother at an early age and lived with his father, a quiet, scholarly man who had apparently turned his back on the world. With the result that Sammy, who was a couple of years older than the twins, was also an odd mixture of wildness and precociousness and, as the twins' bosom companion—he shared their School of the Air lessons—something of a thorn in Serena's side in her efforts to civilise all three.

'That's right,' Cameron piped up. He was normally a step or two behind his brother; he'd been born half an hour later, but could always be relied upon to back Richard up. 'I 'spect it's because Serena's a girl. I mean that's why she's got this thing about being so clean.'

Serena smothered a grin and concentrated on her soup.

'Well,' her employer said with a wry glance at her, 'girls aren't the only clean people, you know. I also clean my ears every day.'

'Yep,' Bill put in, and added conversationally, 'Might be an idea to check Sammy Banks's ears some time. Might find you could plant potatoes in them.'

Cameron giggled, but Richard loked scornful and in no way mollified—as he indicated by returning to the attack, although from an oblique angle.

'You're right, Cameron, can't be much fun being a girl. People *look* at you a lot—noticed that? Maybe that's why they have to worry so much about being clean.'

'They do,' Cameron agreed after some thought. 'Remember the mechanics who flew in to fix the helicopter the other day? One of them looked at Serena so hard he forgot he had a heavy wrench in his hand and dropped it on his toe. What did he say, Richard?'

Serena stiffened as Richard screwed up his face. 'He said—"What's a gorgeous chick like that doing up here beyond the black stump?" Only he swore as well— probably because his toe was hurting.' Richard managed to convey angelic virtue as if he himself would never consider swearing, but also a world-weary acceptance of people who did under provocation. 'Then the other bloke whistled at her. 'Member that, Cameron?'

Serena choked over her soup as Cameron nodded obligingly. 'I remember,' he said slowly, 'because you got cross with Serena. She wouldn't let you go near the helicopter.'

Richard cast his brother a dark glance.

It was Mrs Denby who came to Serena's assistance

unwittingly. 'Richard,' she said thoughtfully, 'I gather you're a little annoyed because Serena sent you back to clean your ears. But you must admit Sean or I would have done the same, so you can't really blame it on the fact that Serena is a girl. In fact you should look on the bright side. At least she's not the kind of girl who minds getting wet and muddy, like the day when two little boys I know pushed her into the creek with her clothes on. Nor does she faint at the sight of frogs in her bed—although I suspect that was rather a disappointment to . . . those same two little boys.'

Richard and Cameron caught each other's eyes, coloured, then burst out laughing. 'No,' Richard said grudgingly at last, 'she took it all like a man, didn't you, Serena?'

Serena was still wondering apprehensively what Sean would make of the helicopter incident and she couldn't resist sending him a fleeting, nervous glance, only to find that he was looking at her with amusement.

She relaxed visibly and turned to Richard. 'Thanks for the compliment, Richard. Does that mean I'm forgiven for being a girl?'

'Of course,' he said boisterously, and changed the subject adroitly, causing Serena still to cherish some doubts about his sincerity. 'Sean, we haven't had a picnic for ages! When can we?'

'I'll think about it,' his uncle promised in perfectly normal tones which encouraged Serena to think the incident was closed. But a little later she looked at him again to find that this time his gaze was resting on her unsmilingly and unreadably, and it sent a shiver down her spine.

And after dinner, when Mrs Denby was pouring the coffee, which they usually drank in the lounge, he said, 'Bring your coffee into the study, will you, Serena. I want to talk to you.'

Her heart sank like a stone.

The silence grew as Serena closed her mouth finally and stared defiantly across the desk.

Sean Wentworth was watching her with a grave expression that warned her of inner amusement, and his eyes were all grey tonight, she noticed angrily. Grey to match his cotton shirt and pincord jeans that fitted him perfectly and set off his tall, broad-shouldered physique admirably. And the tanned column of his throat rose from the open neck of his shirt to the equally tanned contours of his face—a face incredibly hard to read sometimes, and one, she realised, that haunted her somewhat. In the context of that never-to-be-forgotten kiss he had stolen and why, although she had not responded, she had been some-what hypnotised by it. Was it, she had wondered, because of a glimpse of the devastatingly powerful appeal she didn't doubt he would hold for women, matched with a great deal of experience with them, that she had fallen prey to that night?

Yet tonight, that quality was notably absent, and for some reason that she couldn't for the life of her fathom, it annoyed her even more.

'If you've finished laughing at me—and I know you are—may I go?' she asked deliberately. 'Unless of course you don't believe me—which I should be quite used to,' she added bitterly.

He grinned reminiscently and pushed his fingers

through his thick tawny hair as he leant forward.

'Serena, who taught you that attack was the best means of defence?'

'I . . . what do you mean?' she stammered, thrown off balance. 'It's quite true, what I told you! And Cameron confirmed it. We were merely passing by on our way back from a ride and Richard wanted to stop because he's fascinated by mechanical things. But I wouldn't let him because *I* had *no* intention of having anything to do with those two . . . men.' She stuck her chin out haughtily.

'I believe you,' he shrugged, as he toyed with a marble paperweight. 'As a matter of fact that wasn't what I wanted to talk to you about at all, but you didn't give me a chance to get a word in edgeways.'

Serena blinked and subsided rather like a pricked balloon. 'But you looked—in there,' she gestured towards the dining-room, 'I thought you looked cold and as if I were some unpleasant form of sub-life.'

'Dear me,' he drawled, 'I shall have to watch how I look, won't I? Especially as I was going to congratulate you on how well you've handled the twins.'

Serena's eyes widened, but her burning sense of misjustice hadn't faded completely and gave one last flicker. 'I'm surprised you've noticed,' she said, then bit her lip uneasily.

'Oh, I have my ways and means,' he said softly.

'Do you mean . . . people have been spying on me?' she said as the implication of this sank in, and her chin rose again.

'Not spying precisely . . .'

'That sounds . . .'

'Serena, will you be quiet and let me finish!' he

ordered. And waited, favouring her with a grim look.

'I was only going to say—that sounds like something you were rather superior about to me once—not *precisely* lying but doing it by omission. In fact it sounds like *exactly* the same thing to me. But go on.' She folded her hands in her lap and favoured him with a patient expression.

Sean's eyes narrowed and his mouth tightened, then a unwitting glint of amusement lit his eyes and he murmured wryly, '*Touché!* However, my motives were extremely pure. As you've no doubt gathered, the twins are not all joy, so for their sakes and yours I thought it might be . . . expedient, but I didn't want you to feel as if you had someone breathing over your shoulder all the time, waiting to pounce on you if you made a mistake. That kind of thing can be very trying, can't it? But we're all agreed that you've coped well. You've even surprised me, petal,' he added with a quizzical look.

'I have . . . I don't think you should call me that.'

'Why not?'

Serena considered, then said rather confusedly, 'Well, I mean—well, you're supposed to be the architect of my new life, aren't you? How can I reform if you keep reminding me of . . . something I'd rather forget . . .' She broke off and frowned. 'That didn't quite come out right, but . . .'

'I understand, though,' he said with a slight smile. 'Are some things so hard to forget?'

She nodded.

'Such as?' he asked quietly.

'You must know,' she said with a little shrug. 'Such as even being seen dead at the Pelican Club. Have you never made any mistakes in your life? That you find hard to forget?'

'Some,' he said drily. 'But I still find it difficult to visualise the mistake of a magnitude that would place you in such an awkward position. In fact there's really only one that springs to mind, and I suppose such smooth delicate skin and a beautiful little figure together with hair like silk and dark-lashed violet eyes must account for a portion of the responsibility. And yet this is an age of liberation, and even if you did get yourself unwisely pregnant and turfed out of home . . .'

Serena's lips had parted incredulously as he spoke musingly, but now her eyes flashed violet fire, 'Unwisely pregnant! I . . . look . . . well, really,' she said on a shaky breath, 'that's a new one! When did you think that one up? And what do you suppose I've done with the product of this unwise pregnancy? Had it terminated or—no, dumped it down a mine-shaft as in the good old days. How you ca . . .'

'Are you telling me this or . . .'

'I'm telling you *nothing!*' she spat at him. 'I'm . . .'

But he interrupted her coolly, 'My dear, it happens sometimes to the best of us, but often because of,' he shrugged, 'irresponsible men, self-righteous parents —who knows what kind of pressures?—there's some poor unfortunate girl left to carry the burden, whether it's of bearing the child or going through the trauma of an abortion. I may have some faults and you might not like me very much,' his lips twisted, 'but I'm not the kind of person who would hold that against you.'

Serena stared at him, conscious of a feeling of confusion, a feeling of believing him but not wanting to.

Not that it mattered in this context, but in an overall sense, as if her opinions of Sean Wentworth were being unwittingly moulded into something approaching approval—but without her consent, that was the strange thing.

She chewed her lip, frowning, then said with an effort, 'It wasn't—that didn't happen to me. That wasn't why I left . . .' She broke off, then rushed on, 'You *promised* you wouldn't do this, you said . . .'

'I promised I wouldn't do anything about handing you back or actually taking steps such as making enquiries about you. I didn't promise not to wonder and also to wonder if it mightn't help to . . . confide in someone?' Sean's grey gaze held hers steadily.

Serena closed her eyes because, unbelievably, for a moment the temptation to do that was almost over-powering. But . . . She sighed suddenly. 'Thank you, but I'd rather not. I . . . can manage.'

For a moment his mouth hardened, then he lay back in his chair and said, 'All right, that's up to you. There was something else I wanted to talk to you about now that you've served your apprenticeship, in a manner of speaking. The twins' mother is coming up to stay in about a fortnight. One of the reasons you might have encountered some . . . resistance from Richard, at least, is because of her. I——' he sat up and picked up the paperweight thoughtfully '—don't want to burden you with family affairs, but you're obviously not going to be able to avoid them altogether and I think I should warn you that Richard has a . . . history of being diffi-cult, more difficult, when she's lurking on the horizon.'

Once again Serena stared at him with parted lips

until he smiled, but it didn't reach his eyes. 'Don't worry, we'll all be on the alert, and if you just go on the way you have, that's all that's necessary.'

'I . . . see,' Serena said at last. 'I . . . wondered if they had a mother. They've never mentioned her.'

'She and my brother were divorced before he died and although she's free to see them whenever she likes, even have them living with her, she prefers this arrangement for them.'

Serena blinked. 'Oh. Oh, well,' she said feebly, 'thank you for warning me. Does she . . . does she know about me?'

'Of course,' Sean said drily. 'She thoroughly approved of the idea of a governess.' He stood, and Serena did the same because it was obvious the interview was being ended, as he strolled over to the door to open it for her.

But as she went to pass him he put a hand on her shoulder and plucked the sprig of jasmine from her hair and sniffed it. 'In aid of anything special—flowers in your hair?' he queried casually.

Serena stiffened and had to tilt her head back to look up at him because they were standing so close. 'No,' she said shortly.

He tucked the sprig back in. 'You're very prickly,' he drawled. 'I only meant—were they in aid of a——' he shrugged '—birthday you forgot to tell us about or something like that?'

'Oh.' Serena bit her lip. 'No. I . . . just felt happy when I was getting dressed.'

'And now I've gone and made you unhappy? I'm sorry.' He finished adjusting the jasmine and touched the point of her chin with his fingers. 'It seems I'll have to try to reform, too. Goodnight, Serena. Thank you for all the trouble you've taken with Richard and Cameron and I'm sorry for all the discomfort you've had to bear. They're . . . very precious to me.'

Serena found it very difficult to get to sleep that night. Mainly because she couldn't help mulling over her conversation with Sean but also because—yes, she had to admit it, she was dying of curiosity about this mysterious mother who had left her sons to Sean's care. Not that she would dream of asking anyone about her . . .

It was Mrs Denby, a couple of days later, who filled Serena in without having to be asked. For some reason she had attacked the house in a flurry of spring-cleaning and was going around looking worried and flustered, a state so far removed from her normal attitude to life that on this particular morning Serena, coming upon her minutely scouring some some already dazzling pots, removed them from her, propelled her gently towards a kitchen chair and commanded her to relax while she made them a cup of tea.

'That's very kind of you, my dear,' Mrs Denby said as she sank down. 'I can't imagine how I ever got along without you!'

Serena smiled at her. 'Is something the matter?'

'No. Why?' Mrs Denby asked hastily.

'You've cleaned this place within an inch of its life, and it was already clean.'

'I . . .' Mrs Denby grimaced and sighed. 'It's my way of working off my tensions, I guess.'

'I didn't know you had any. Want to tell me?' Serena sat down opposite her and poured the tea.

Mrs Denby hesitated. 'It's . . . Delvene, I guess.'

'Delvene?'

'Mrs Andrew Wentworth—for all that she might have renounced that title. She's coming up in a fortnight.'

'Oh! The twins' mother? Yes, Sean told me.'

'He did?' Mrs Denby looked relieved.

'What's she like?' asked Serena.

'She's . . . beautiful, but perhaps I ought to warn you, Serena . . .'

'If you're going to say what I think you are, Sean's already done that too. About Richard.'

'Oh, good. Much better for you to be in the know, although, naturally, Sean doesn't like broadcasting our problems.'

'Naturally,' murmured Serena. 'It must be very awkward,' she added with a frown. 'Why . . . does she leave them here?'

Mrs Denby sighed again. 'It's a long, sad story, Serena. Delvene is a dancer, and a very good one, to give her credit. She started out as a ballet dancer, then she turned a modern dance, and she's the principal dancer of a quite famous company now. And to put matters in a nutshell, she married Andrew when she was young—and poor—although I must say they seemed to be very much in love, but not many months later they were fighting like cat and dog. He wanted to live here as he'd always done, she wanted to live in Sydney and to keep on dancing. He wasn't much of a match for her, unfortunately, although he was such a honey, Andrew.' Mrs Denby wiped away a tear with the corner of her apron.

'What happened?'

Mrs Denby studied her hands. 'He gave in,' she said at last. 'But a couple of years later, they were divorced and Andrew came home—with the twins. And even after he died, Delvene was quite content to continue that arrangement with Sean. What . . . what would you think of a woman like that?' she asked sadly.

Truth to tell, Serena was lost for words.

'Of course,' Mrs Denby went on honestly, 'with her life-style the way it is, they're much better off here, and she does come to see them frequently, but . . .' She broke off and shrugged helplessly.

'They're getting to an age where they don't just accept these things,' Serena said thoughtfully. 'I see.'

'Cameron still thinks she's marvellous and Richard used to, but now he won't talk about her, and they had a silver-framed photo of her in their bedroom which he hides when she leaves.'

'I *wondered* why . . . oh dear,' sighed Serena. 'Does Sean know this?'

'Yes, and that's why . . . you see, we generally go out of our way to make things as normal as possible when she's here, I mean, as if the divorce never happened, but this time I've got the feeling Sean won't be so . . . well, you might know what I mean.'

'Yes,' Serena agreed with feeling. Then she coloured faintly and said quickly, 'But if she has this talent . . .' She stopped and started again. 'Some people, when they have a talent or an art, just can't ignore it. It's like a force inside them they can't deny. She . . .'

'That's true,' Mrs Denby broke in. 'You can see it in her hands, the way she walks, her energy and vitality—how wise you are for someone so young, Serena,' she said with a smile, then added ruefully, 'Unfortunately it's a little difficult for us to be . . . unbiased about Delvene.'

'Are they like her—Richard and Cameron?' Serena asked curiously.

'Well, it's an odd mixture,' said Mrs Denby. 'They're a lot like Andrew—it quite tears my heart out sometimes, and Sean's, I think, and Cameron seems to have inherited his father's nature: gentle, thoughtful, a bit of a daydreamer.'

'And Richard?'

'Richard, my dear,' Mrs Denby said, as she gathered up the tea cups, 'is a straight blend of Delvene and Sean with a few original quirks thrown in for good measure. Dynamite, in other words—you might have noticed?'

Serena laughed. 'It's not that I mind the frogs in my bed or the mice in my drawers so *much*, it's that clear, piercing look he gives me every now and then. As if he's looking right through me—you're right, Sean does the same!'

They grinned at each other. Then Mrs Denby sobered. 'Sean and Andrew used to be very close,' she remarked, and was silent for a time. 'Oh, well, thanks for listening, Serena. I hope I haven't told you anything you'd rather not have known, but I feel a bit better!'

Serena kept a hawk-like watch over Richard as the days passed, but as it happened, her vigilance was not proof against his state of mind.

The month of March was slipping away towards

April and the nights were drawing in earlier and with a chilliness about them. Serena was thinking about this as she and the twins were coming home from an afternoon ride.

She glanced at her watch and said, 'We mustn't dawdle, fellas. It'll be dark soon.'

'I know my way around here blindfolded,' Richard informed her with an air of patronage.

'That's because we're not far from the house,' Cameron offered. 'I do too. Oh, Serena!' He pulled up his pony. 'See that? Can't I just get down and have a closer look?' he pleaded.

'It's only an old frilly lizard,' Richard said impatiently. 'You must have seen hundreds of them!'

'Please, Serena,' Cameron begged.

Serena hesitated. While Richard's passion in life was for things mechanical, Cameron's was for any sort of reptile life. 'All right,' she said. 'Just a quick look, mind!' And she obligingly slipped off her horse. 'I must say he's the biggest one I've ever seen. Look at him puffing himself up!' she added wonderingly as they cautiously approached the low rock on which the creature was lying.

'Wow!' Cameron breathed. 'Hey, Richie . . .'

But both he and Serena spun round at the sound of galloping hooves, and it was with twin gasps of dismay that they saw Richard disappearing in a cloud of dust, in the opposite direction to the house.

'Where . . . where's he going?' Serena demanded of his twin.

Cameron slid his hand into Serena's. 'He's not allowed to do that,' he said in a small voice. 'He shouldn't go off on his own. He'll get into big trouble.'

Serena took a deep breath. 'Cameron, *does* he know his way around out there?'

'N-not in the dark,' said Cameron with a tremor in his voice. 'Sean will belt him for this. We shouldn't have stopped. What will we do, Serena?'

'Cameron,' she said gravely, 'now you must promise me you'll do exactly as I say. Hop up.'

They both mounted and Serena led the way over a low ridge from where the homestead was visible.

'Now you must ride straight home, Cameron.'

'But what will I tell Sean when I get there?' Cameron asked tearfully.

'Just tell him,' Serena said soothingly, 'that Richard's pony got a fright and bolted with him. You can describe to him where we were and the direction Richard went. All right?'

Cameron nodded with relief.

Serena went on, 'Now it's going to be dark before long, so you must tell Sean or Mrs Denby as *soon* as you get home and tell them I've gone after him. I'm pretty sure the horses know their way home, so we should be fine, but just in case—I'm depending on you!' She ruffled his fair hair.

'I'll ride like the wind!' Cameron promised.

'Well, better to take it steadily—we don't want to lose both of you. Off you go!'

Cameron did as he was bid and Serena turned her horse, only to be shortly aware that either she didn't have the way with horses Richard had, or else the unprepossessing one she'd chosen from the saddle paddock that afternoon was more interested in heading home to the evening ration of lucerne that awaited him. Whichever it was, he was a reluctant conveyance, and as the sun started to set with a fiery splendour, the small dot that was Richard seemed to disappear into it.

It was a large kangaroo that settled the dispute between Serena and her horse. It hopped out curiously from a stand of spindly mulgas, the horse shied and reared, and Serena fell off heavily, to lie stunned for a moment or two. The horse made the most of this opportunity and set off briskly for home.

Her first thought as she came to was an irrational one . . .

'Serves you right, Serena, for encouraging Cameron to tell lies. Is Sean ever going to believe that two horses took fright and bolted?'

She stood up slowly, then sat down suddenly, realising she was still groggy, and stared around helplessly. The landscape was indescribably beautiful as the light faded. A symphony of rose-coloured tones on the sandy soil, a stark white tree trunk beneath the darkening sky and then, before her eyes, it was all overlaid as if she was viewing a coloured negative. The living tints started to fade as twilight took over.

She shivered suddenly and got up more determinedly this time. It was going to be a fairly painful walk and she wasn't sure how much further she was from the homestead, but judged it at least another mile despite her horse's tardy progress. She'd be lucky to make it before dark fell completely, but she would have the lights to guide her. But it was the thought of Richard that made her quicken her step. Richard, who reminded everyone so much of his dead father despite his different nature.

'Dear God,' she muttered out loud, 'if I've lost Richard will they ever forgive me?'

Serena never knew how she managed to get lost.

In fact it was only after she had been walking for well over an hour that she admitted as much to herself.

But I can't have passed the house, she thought tearfully, as she sank to the ground. Unless, because I was still a bit groggy, I changed direction very gradually without realising it . . . I could be anywhere!

She sat with her head between her knees for five minutes trying to calm herself.

'If only there was a moon,' she whispered despondently. But when she looked up there was not even a star. 'Clouded over,' she added to herself, and jumped as two things hit her simultaneously. One was a large raindrop and the other was the recollection that rain had been forecast for the latter part of the day. In this area where every drop of rain was precious, most of its inhabitants were avid followers of the radio weather reports, and she had heard Sean and Bill discussing the possibility of rain earlier in the day.

'Oh, no,' she groaned as more drops fell. 'Why tonight? I mean, I know they want rain, but does it have to be tonight of all nights?'

The rain was gentle, almost tentative at first, and she sighed with relief, thinking it might be only a passing shower. She stood up and peered around for a more comfortable spot to sit and took a few steps forward, to find the ground sloping gently away, and a large boulder. She felt around it and decided she could lean back against it and even get some protection from the rain, but for good measure, she walked all around it, jumping up and down and scuffing the soil with her boots. 'There,' she told herself, 'no self-respecting snake would stay around after that!' And she sank down wearily.

It was as if this was an invisible signal to the heavens above, because without further warning all tentativeness was abandoned as they opened up and tipped their contents on to Serena in what felt like a solid sheet of water.

There was nothing she could do but crouch there with the rain hammering down, not only soaked to the skin but aware that the ground around her was getting waterlogged.

She lost count of time, but finally, after what seemed like hours, the rain eased to a slight drizzle and she was able to stand up, a desolate, sodden figure, only to realise that she was standing ankle-deep in a flowing stream of water. A large moon chose that moment to swim out from behind a cloud, to reveal a further frightening fact to her. The stream seemed to be widening before her eyes. She gasped in real fear as the implication of this hit her. She'd wandered into a dried-up creek bed—only it was no longer dry at all.

The next few minutes were like some nightmare. At each step she took, she seemed to slip back two as the water swirled and clutched at her boots. She slipped once and had to claw her way up a small bank that was fast becoming submerged too. And when she saw the light, she thought at first that the moon had swung round her somehow—or that she'd done it again, lost all sense of direction.

Then, whimpering and scrabbling furiously, she suddenly realised that it was no moon but a dazzling spotlight.

'Oh, thank God!' she cried, falling and not bothering to get up but crawling forward on her hands and knees. For behind that light there had to be a safe, solid four-wheel-drive vehicle and someone to help her—if only they could see her!

'Help!' she shouted. 'Oh, please, don't go away, I'm here . . . oh, thank heavens!' this as a dark figure loomed up in front of her, and she stood up precariously and threw herself into a pair of waterproof-clad arms, uncaring and oblivious of who it was and with but one thought on her mind. 'Richard,' she panted. 'We must find Richard . . .'

Without a word her rescuer picked her up and slung her over his shoulder. She was still babbling incoherently as a few strides brought them around behind the spotlight which was indeed fixed to a long-bodied Land Rover and she was bundled none too ceremoniously into the back of it. Then he climbed in after her and fumbled for a moment before switching on a powerful torch, and Serena found herself staring into Sean Wentworth's cold grey eyes.

Her lips parted and she closed her eyes wearily. 'I'm so sorry,' she murmured, and slumped back against a spare tyre.

But the feel of his hands on her shoulders caused her lashes to fly up.

He jerked her upright. 'So you ought to be! You could have *died* in any one of several ways. Not to mention all the trouble you've put us to—which is not over yet, incidentally.'

'You haven't found him?' she whispered, staring fearfully at a nerve beating in his jaw.

He swore then and she flinched as his fingers dug into her shoulders. 'Richard,' he said grimly, 'arrived home safe and sound not long after dusk because he had the sense to stick with his horse and let it find its own way home.'

For a moment Serena was too relieved to speak, which afforded Sean the opportunity to continue harshly, 'Whereas you, a newcomer to Rosewood of all people, didn't even stop to think that you would have the least chance of finding him!'

'I . . . I was going to let my horse find its way home after I'd scouted around a bit,' said Serena with a spark of defiance. 'I'm not that stupid, only . . .'

'Only you couldn't even stay on it,' he said contemptuously.

Her tongue seemed to tie itself into knots before she was able to say hotly, 'That wasn't my fault! It's the most stupid horse I've ever ridden, and I notice *you* don't get around on a pigheaded, obstinate nag with nothing in his head but the thought of tucker!' she flung at him, referring to the beautiful black gelding that was reserved for his sole use.

'That's beside the point,' he said coldly. 'And then, to make matters worse, instead of staying put where we would have found you hours ago, you had to walk bloody miles and straight into this channel country in a bloody cloudburst!' He shook her angrily.

'I didn't . . . deliberately walk into this,' she stammered, 'but I must have been groggy after I fell off and . . . don't!' she pleaded as her head jerked back again. 'You're hurting me . . .'

Sean stopped shaking her and stared down at her. 'It's what you need,' he said roughly. 'If I had any sense I'd put you over my knee and beat the living daylights out of you just to teach you to stop and think before you jump into these rash acts you seem so addicted to. You *do* realise you could have drowned, among other things, Serena, don't you?'

'I—yes,' she said through trembling lips. 'I'm very sorry.' She brushed at the tears in her eyes. 'I only thought of finding him, that's all.'

He took a breath and some of the tension seemed to seep out of him, then with a muttered exclamation as she started to cry in earnest, unable to contain the sobs that rose to her throat any longer, he drew her into his arms.

'All right,' he said on a gentler note. 'It's over now, kid.'

But it seemed it wasn't all over for Serena as a sort of hysterical reaction set in, and try as she might, she couldn't stop her tears or the painful shudders that racked her body as she sobbed distractedly into his damp shirtfront.

'Hey,' he said finally, 'that's enough.' He eased her away from him and eyed her with a grin. 'You look like a drowned rabbit anyway, but this is only making it worse!'

Serena choked on her sobs and twisted away from him distraughtly, but when she heard him laugh almost beneath his breath, she clenched her fists and called on every ounce of will-power she possessed in an effort to regain some composure. Finally, the racking sobs subsided and she was able to turn to him, to see that he was studying her with a mocking little glint in his eyes just as if he was recalling another occasion when he had rescued her damp, dirty, bedraggled person.

Serena looked down at herself and sighed exasperatedly as she pulled a wet hanky from her pocket and blew her nose. 'I hate you,' she said almost conversationally. 'I know what you're thinking, and what beats me is why it always has to be *you*. Why couldn't Bill have found me tonight?'

'That would only have delayed the scolding,' he said mildly. 'But talking of Bill, it's about time I let him know you're safe and sound. He's at the house co-ordinating the search.'

This was accomplished through a two-way radio with which the Land Rover was equipped, and although Serena had resolved not even to look at her employer again, she couldn't help it when she heard the conversation he had with Bill.

In fact she was staring at him open-mouthed when he signed off.

'All night?' she said incredulously. 'Do you mean we're stuck here all night?'

'I don't see why you should be so surprised,' he replied ironically. 'You all but drowned in one channel, and there's now an even deeper one flowing between us and the house. We are, in a word, trapped. For the time being.'

'But . . . but this is a Land Rover!' she stammered.

'Precisely.' He shrugged. 'It can't sprout wings, nor does it float, so we have no option but to stick to this piece of high ground until daylight, and if the creeks haven't subsided by then, they can get us out with the helicopter, but I don't think that will be necessary. From all the information Bill has now, this was a fairly isolated downpour. If it doesn't rain any more up-country, by the morning the earth will have soaked up the water like blotting paper. Er . . . I think it's time you got out of those wet clothes. You're sitting in a puddle of water.'

'Thank you, but I'll stay in them,' she retorted.

'No, you won't,' Sean said evenly, and leant towards her. 'Once the clouds clear it will get a lot colder. You're only inviting a chill.'

'You're very thoughtful all of a sudden, but apart from anything else, I don't have anything to change into and . . .'

'Oh yes, you do.' He reached over to the front seat and produced a wicker basket. 'Denny threw in some emergency rations.' He withdrew a thermos flask and a plastic container. 'And some dry clothes for you as well as a towel.' He tossed a clean pair of jeans and a flannel shirt into her lap.

Serena looked down at them and then back at him, her expression mutinous. 'I'm not changing with you sitting there!'

'I won't look,' he said with his lips quirking.

'You're so right,' she said hotly, 'because there'll be nothing to see. If you want me to change you can get out in the rain again.' And she added even more explosively, 'Are you *sure* we have to stay here all night?'

'Serena,' he said with dangerous quiet, 'I'll explain it to you just once more. This is treacherous country in these conditions. It's a maze of channels and creek beds all littered with holes and rocks and tree stumps. Even in broad daylight it would be no easy matter to get home. Now will you take those wet clothes off or must I?'

'I wondered when we'd come to that,' she murmured, not quite sure what had prompted her, but it seemed her guard was for ever up in this matter now.

The effect of her words was unexpected. Sean muttered something unintelligible and hauled her forward so that she was half sitting, half kneeling in front of him, and said irately, 'If you imagine I set this all up so I could take unfair advantage of you, banish the thought. In case your memory stops short, I knocked back a golden opportunity so to do once before. And if you're just being stubborn, allow me to show you once again what little effect your immature, schoolgirlish charms have on me.'

'No!' she gasped, and twisted away, at the same time trying to push his hands away as he started to unbutton her blouse. 'Don't! How dare . . . you,' she cried incoherently.

'I'll tell you why I dare,' he said silkily as he deftly removed her blouse and bra despite her panting exertions and flicked a cool, impersonal glance at her breasts as she tried desperately to cover herself up, 'because I'm stronger than you, because pneumonia is the last thing we need and because I'm quite unmoved by your outraged maidenly modesty. Here.' He handed her the towel. 'Use it!' he commanded as she went to wrap herself in it.

Serena closed her eyes, going hot and cold by turns, and rubbed herself feverishly, her face burning with embarrassment.

'Right,' he said, and removed the towel from her fingers and handed her the blouse, which she scrambled into and started to button up crookedly.

'Hang on,' he ordered, and impatiently removed her useless, dithering fingers to button her efficiently up to the chin. Then he said, 'You may do the rest, so long as you acknowledge something before we go one step further.'

Her eyes were wide and wary.

'That I have no intention of raping you or seducing you in any way, Serena.' His eyes were cold.

'I . . . all right,' she said sulkily. 'But I still hate you.'

'I know,' he agreed gravely, although the hard lines of his face softened. 'But you probably feel better hating me than being scared out of your wits. Believe it or not, I think it's stopped raining.' He paused and they both listened, and it had. 'I'll step out and take a look around while you do the rest.'

Serena was galvanised into action as he peered out into the darkness, then jumped down. She completed her change quickly and used her wet clothes to mop up the puddle on the floor as best she could. Then she started to rub her wet hair just as Sean climbed back in.

Their eyes met briefly, but she looked away first and concentrated on drying her hair. A flicker of a smile touched his lips, but all he said was, 'Hungry?' and reached for the plastic box.

Serena rubbed for a moment longer, then folded the towel very carefully. 'Sean?'

'Uh-huh?'

'I am sorry,' she said lamely. 'For being such a bother, and I don't want you to think I'm not grateful to you for rescuing me.'

His grey-green eyes glinted with laughter, although he said solemnly, 'Thank you,' and pulled the lid off the box to reveal a golden, cold roast chicken, some buttered rolls and three wedges of apple pie. 'Tuck in,' he invited.

Serena hesitated, folding the towel ever smaller.

'Now surely this agony of remorse hasn't affected your appetite?' he queried, and handed her a chicken leg.

She stared at it, then lifted her eyes to his and smiled tremulously suddenly. 'I'm starving,' she admitted. 'Just starving!'

A little while later, Serena licked her fingers unashamedly and said dreamily, 'That was terrific. Are you sure you didn't want that last piece of apple pie?'

'Quite sure.' Sean unscrewed the thermos. 'Think you could fit in some coffee?'

She nodded and started to tidy up as he drew a silver flask from the basket and added a generous dollop of its contents to the plastic mug he offered her. 'Brandy,' he said briefly to her look of enquiry. 'It might make you sleep.'

She wrinkled her nose as she sipped the hot liquid thoughtfully. 'It's a bit strong,' she said with a glimmer of a smile, but sipped some more, then settled herself more comfortably. 'Do you know something?'

'No. What?' He'd stretched his long legs out and was leaning up on one elbow. He had turned the flashlight off and lit a small gas lantern that gave off a dim, warm glow from its hook on the roof and left shadows in the corners.

'I like this part of the world.'

'I'm . . . glad to hear you say so.' He sounded polite and amused.

Serena took another draught of her coffee and ignored the amusement. 'Yes, I do. It makes me feel—I don't know—as if I'm exploring the heart of Australia. I feel, even though we live in a house, as if I'm on safari and as if every day is going to be an exciting one. Do you feel that?' She drained her cup and handed it to him for a refill. 'I mean,' she went on, not wating for him to answer, 'you read about Cooper Creek and the Diamantina and Georgina Rivers and great artesian basins, mulgas and emus and Major Mitchell . . .' she blinked as he laced her coffee again, but didn't protest, 'cockatoos. Thanks.' She sipped reflectively. 'But actually being here is rather fantastic.'

'We're a bit south of the Diamantina,' he said gravely. 'It's the Warrego and Paroo that feed this corner of Queensland.'

'Oh, well,' Serena waved a hand dismissively, 'I don't really mind. They sound just as good. Do you feel like that? Or do you get used to it if you've lived here all your life?'

'Not . . . altogether,' Sean said idly, his eyes on her unconscious face, alive with wonder in the soft light.

'That's good . . . You know, I always wanted to see this part of the world—actually I'd love to see all of off-beat Australia. The Birdsville Track, the Nullabor when it's a carpet of wild flowers, Lake Eyre—so many places.' She drained her mug and stared unseeing at the canvas wall as if she could picture all those vistas. Then she yawned and hiccuped at the same time. 'Oh, dear,' she said ruefully. 'Do you think I'm tipsy?'

His lips twitched and he sat up and opened a long

in box from which he extracted a thick coil of rope, several tools and finally two rolled-up sleeping bags, some blankets and two rather flat pillows covered in grey and white ticking. He put the rope and tools back and answered her finally. 'Ready for bed, probably.'

'Actually, I wouldn't mind a drop more,' Serena said as she watched him lay the sleeping bags out and tucked her feet beneath her to get out of the way. 'It's very . . . soothing.'

'I wouldn't advise it. Strange things can happen when you're tipsy. You might even find you don't hate me any more. Try that,' he invited as he removed her empty cup from her fingers. 'Lie on top of the sleeping bag. It'll be softer and we've got two blankets each.'

Serena lay down thankfully because she was quite suddenly very sleepy. 'Mmm,' she murmured, as he covered her with the blankets, 'it's like home from home. You know,' she yawned again, 'I'm sure I *could* like you if we hadn't met in such awful circumstances. You're a very . . . dependable person to know and you're very . . . straight, which I admire in people. Well, except for that once, but even so I do find I can't help trusting you . . .'

She didn't complete her drowsy, rambling remarks as she fell asleep with her cheek cradled in one hand.

Sean stared down at her with a quizzically raised eyebrow for a long moment. Then he adjusted the blankets around her and lay down himself. 'Sweet dreams—you impossible child,' he murmured.

Serena woke slowly.

She could see it was daylight through a split in the canvas, but she lay still for a while, adjusting her mind

to a curious circumstance which she gradually realised
was that she was lying rather comfortably cradled in
her employer's arms.

She sat up hurriedly but was unable to suppress a
heartfelt groan.

'What is it?' Sean sat up himself, pushing his hair
off his forehead and rubbing the blue shadows on his
jaw. 'What's the matter? Don't you feel well?' His
glance sharpened as he took in her pink cheeks.

'I feel fine,' she said primly.

'Why the groan, then . . .? Oh,' he smiled faintly,
'that was only a . . . brotherly embrace to keep us both
warm, I can assure you. After what you said last night
I didn't think you'd mind.'

Serena bit her lip as she tried to remember what
she'd said last, and coming up with a hazy
recollection of telling him she trusted him. And
remembering also that it had got very cold during
the night and that she'd half woken, shivering, and
actually reached out . . .

'It wasn't that,' she said hastily. 'If you must know,
I feel as stiff as a board.'

'Well, I'd hate to imagine what feeling unwell
would be like if that's feeling fine, but it's also not so
surprising,' he said with a shrug. 'Perhaps you should
go into training before you undertake a cross-country
hike after falling off your horse the next time.'

This silenced Serena effectively, although she
flashed him a dark look. But when he helped her out of
the Land Rover and pointed out a convenient clump of
bushes, the sparkling, diamond-clear scene that met
her eyes banished all her irritation. The earth was still
damp, but the sky and the mulga scrub and the flat-

topped acacia trees were all standing out with a vivid, startling clarity in the cool, early morning air.

She breathed deeply at the beauty of it as well as the unexpectedness. 'I can't believe it,' she said wonderingly. 'Last night I was sure I was going to drown. Where did all the water go?'

'I told you, it takes a lot more than what we had to really flood this country. We should be able to get home without having to be rescued.'

All the same, it was a difficult drive in the still soggy conditions, and the journey home was one of few words as Sean concentrated on his driving and Serena drank in the beauty of it all.

But as they got closer to the homestead, she stopped staring about enchantedly, and realised with a touch of foreboding that Sean wasn't now in a particularly good mood. This caused her to feel guilty for having been such a nuisance and she tried to apologise again, but he cut her short with an abrupt gesture.

'Don't worry about it. One thing, though, what did cause Richard's horse to bolt?'

She chewed her lip. 'It . . . was a kangaroo.'

He turned his head and his eyes held hers for what seemed like an age, and when he finally switched his gaze back to the landscape they were crossing, she felt her heart start to beat uncomfortably.

He said, 'I appreciate that you're trying to cover for Richard, but I'd appreciate it much more if you didn't fine it quite so easy to tell lies.'

'I never find it easy to tell lies,' she retorted, then grimaced secretly and added cautiously, 'How do you know I'm lying anyway?'

'Cameron told me it was a snake and Richard said it

was a goanna. Someone has to be lying,' Sean said expressionlessly.

Serena thought for a moment before she said slowly, 'There are lies and lies. For that matter, I don't appreciate being led into a trap like that. But I do think you should allow me to handle this in my own way. And I lied to you because I'm sure Richard is expecting me to dob him in. Is that such a despicable lie to tell?'

'Serena, so far as Richard is concerned, I'd far rather be wholly within your confidence. In fact that's an order.'

'Belting him isn't going to help the problem,' she said hotly.

'Who said I was going to belt him?' he asked grimly.

'C . . .' Serena stopped short and started again. 'You offered to beat the living daylights out of me only last night!'

'That's because you're old enough to know better. Or should be. Now just listen to me,' he commanded as she opened her mouth, 'before you start getting carried away and telling me you hate me again, I appreciate that you did what you did with the very best of intentions. I also am all for your gaining Richard's confidence and I won't do anything to disrupt the process unnecessarily. But I want to know exactly what's going on at all times.'

The way he said it caused Serena to shiver, but she was silent.

'Serena?'

She took a breath. 'All right,' she said reluctantly. 'What are you going to do about last night? He . . . do you remember how I wouldn't let him watch them fix the helicopter? Well, last night, Cameron wanted to stop and have a look at a frilly lizard, which might have seemed a bit unfair to Richard, so . . . so he galloped off. It was getting late—and it was my horse that bolted because of a kangaroo after getting rid of me, but it would have found some other excuse, I'm sure.'

'I see. All right, I'll do nothing this time. In any case, when he realised *you* were lost, he got a nasty fright, so we'll let it lie. Just don't ever lose your sense of proportion about Richard, Serena.'

'I won't,' she promised, and it struck her that the reason for Sean's change of mood might have more to do with Richard than herself. And his errant sister-in-law who was due shortly . . .

She was silent for the rest of the drive, trying to visualise Delvene and wondering, in view of how she had treated his brother and his nephews, just how Sean treated *her*. In private, naturally, but all the same . . .

'What's the matter now?'

'Nothing.' Serena came out of her reverie and stared at him.

'You shivered, and not only that, you looked . . .' he shrugged, 'extremely apprehensive.'

'I . . . I was . . . er—well, I wouldn't like to tell you another lie so early in the morning, but I don't think I can tell you the truth because it's really none of my business, so . . .'

Sean raised his eyes heavenwards and cut in drily, 'Never mind. We're home, as it happens.' He brought the Land Rover to a halt at the garden fence and added briefly, 'Out you get.'

'What about you? You haven't had any breakfast . . .'

'I'll survive. There's a mob of steers I want to check

first. Will you just do as you're told for once, Serena!'

She did, in hurt silence, and didn't see him grit his teeth in exasperation before he drove off, spinning the wheels of the Land Rover in the mud.

CHAPTER FOUR

MUCH to her disgust, Mrs Denby insisted on treating Serena as an invalid for the rest of the day.

'But I'm fine!' she protested when Mrs Denby commanded her to soak in a warm bath to which she had personally added a mysterious selection of powders.

'If you're you so fine, why do you stop to think before you take a step? Now just do as I say, Serena, or I'll get Sean back to deal with you,' Denny threatened.

Serena hastened to comply.

But as she lay in the soothing bath, she found her thoughts taking an unexpected turn . . . Do I have such a schoolgirlish, immature figure? she wondered. Or did he just mean my . . . whole aura?

And when she finally stepped out, she paused as she was drying herself, to examine her figure critically in the mirror. Her breasts were certainly not large, and at one stage during her adolescence this had been a cause for concern. But they were delicately rounded now and her waist was tiny and her hips had subtly acquired a trim yet also rounded shape.

'. . . And he did *once* say something about a beautiful little figure,' she mused, 'so it must be my aura. Either that or he likes his women bustier and taller, perhaps.'

She stood there deep in thought for a time, then closed her eyes as a strange feeling of confusion stole over her, strange yet strangely familiar, and it was with suddenly pink cheeks that she quickly got dressed.

Richard and Cameron were also insistent on keeping her company when Mrs Denby would allow it, fetching and carrying for her as she rested on her bed, and Richard offered to read her a story.

Serena studied him covertly as he read haltingly. There was no doubt he was subdued, and every now and then he looked at her expectantly, as if the suspense was killing him. Cameron kept touching her hand and looking as if he would like to throw his arms around her neck.

She said gravely as Richard closed the book, 'Boys, I think we need to talk.'

Richard's clear gaze leapt from the book to her face. 'Did you tell him?' he asked straightly.

'I had to. He knew one of us was lying because we all got our stories mixed up. He's not going to do anything this time, although,' she paused, 'he was very cross with me.'

Richard frowned. 'With you!'

'Yes. You see, it's my job to look after you, not to get myself lost and cause everyone so much trouble.'

'But that's not fair!' Richard protested hotly.

'Well, it is in a way. What started it all—you wanting to disobey me—means we're not getting along very well, and *that* means I'm not doing my job properly—do you see? And if it keeps happening, Sean is going to think of getting rid of me and getting someone else. Is that . . . what you want?' Serena gazed at him.

'I . . . no,' Richard said confusedly. 'Course not,' he added gruffly, then turned unexpectedly to Cameron. 'Why don't you go and get Serena another cup of coffee?' he demanded. 'This one's gone cold.'

Cameron looked taken aback, but he went none the less, although with a stern admonition not to discuss anything further until he got back.

Serena narrowed her eyes as Richard slipped off the bed and closed the door softly. 'What is it you don't want Cameron to hear?' she queried as he came back to the bed.

Richard sighed heavily. 'We did . . . I mean, when we heard we were getting a *girl* to look after us,' he said with heavy sarcasm, then stopped and looked at her helplessly.

'I think I understand,' she said after a moment. 'I suppose that's why you put all those frogs and things in my bed?'

Richard coloured faintly. 'Sammy Banks reckoned you'd faint clean away when we put that gecko in your slipper. But you don't seem to be like girls are supposed to be, do you? You even kept him for a pet,' he said aggrievedly.

'Well, I'm sorry to disappoint Sammy Banks,' Serena said somewhat grimly as she recalled the ever-increasing size and horde of wildlife that had taken to haunting her room, 'but I'll tell you something, Richard. If I find so much as a stray ant in here from now on, I'll not only box your ears but

Sammy Banks's too. And don't think I wouldn't. You haven't seen me really mad yet!'

Richard stared at her consideringly. Then he said, 'OK. What about the gecko?' He pointed up to the ceiling.

Serena shrugged. 'He can stay. I can handle him—so, you wanted to frighten the life out of me at first because you thought you were too old to have a girl governess. All right, but then what? Did you plan to make Sean get cross with me so that he'd send me away?'

Richard looked perplexed. 'I didn't *plan* it really. But . . . I got cross last night and wished you would go away.'

'Because I let Cameron stop for the frilly lizard but I wouldn't let you stop to see the helicopter being fixed?'

Richard chewed his lip. 'It wasn't very fair, but . . . it's Cameron.'

'Cameron?'

'Yes. He's getting soft on you,' Richard said fiercely. 'He *wants* you to stay, but I heard the blacksmith telling Bill that a girl like you would get tired of it in a couple of months and he didn't know what Sean musta been thinking. Cameron . . . after Mum's been, he cries into his pillow. He doesn't think I know. So what's going to happen after he gets to like you even more and you leave?'

Violet eyes stared into angry blue ones as Serena sorted through Richard's speech, then she said softly, 'I see. Richard, I'd like to be able to tell you that I plan to stay for years, certainly longer than a few months, but I couldn't guarantee it. Things can change . . .'

'Would you really?'

'Yes, I would.' Serena smiled wryly at him. 'The other thing is, little by little Cameron will grow up and he'll find he won't need someone like me so much, and he'll also be able to understand better—about your mother. You could find you will, too,' she said carefully. 'So in the meantime, I think the best thing to do is not to worry so much—that's all we can do.'

'Don't tell him I told you this!' Richard warned hastily as Cameron could be heard approaching.

'Of course I won't. Will *you* try . . . not to get cross and do awkward things?'

He shrugged. 'I'll *try*. I can't promise anything.'

And with that Serena had to be content as Cameron entered, his tongue sticking out slightly with the effort of not spilling the coffee.

'Why, thank you, Cameron,' she said, taking the cup from him. 'Did you make this all by yourself?' She groaned inwardly as Cameron nodded and climbed on to her bed to join his brother, but she sipped the pale, anaemic brew heroically.

The next morning saw her feeling a lot better, although a little wary in that she hadn't seen Sean since he'd dumped her at the garden fence.

Then Bill announced that he was taking the twins and Sammy Banks for a joyride, that Sean had okayed it, and that she should relax for the morning.

'But I'm perfectly all right!' she protested.

'Boss's orders,' Bill said laconically, and Richard and Cameron gave her to understand she should definitely rest and relax, they were all in favour of it.

'I can imagine,' she murmured. 'Er . . . speaking of the boss, where is he? He didn't have dinner last night.'

'Got home late. Out and about today.' And with those sparse comments from Bill, she had to be content.

Nor would Mrs Denby accept her offers of assistance with the housework. 'You go and . . . read a book, Serena,' she said. 'You deserve a bit of time off, love.'

As it happened, Serena, who normally loved reading, couldn't find a single book that interested her, so she tidied out her drawers, washed out some of her beautiful lacy underwear, then sat on her part of the veranda, forlornly staring out over the garden and feeling as if she'd been sent to Coventry.

'He was annoyed with me,' she whispered to herself. 'I could tell—I mean, that he found me very tiresome. Is this his way of punishing me? I would have loved to have gone on a joyride with Bill and the kids instead of . . . this.'

So wrapped up was she in her depressing reverie, she didn't hear the sound of horses cantering up to the main gate which was on the other side of the house, nor did she hear footsteps through the house and the murmur of voices. And she didn't realise that her employer had entered her bedroom through the other door, had crossed the room silently on the carpet and was standing just inside the French doors observing her sad profile with a lift of his eyebrow.

So the first intimation she had that she was not

alone came when he said, 'What's this? You look as if you're attending a secret wake!'

Serena jumped and went scarlet. 'I . . . I didn't hear you,' she stammered.

'You were certainly deep in thought.' His lips twitched. 'Am I allowed to know what about this time?'

Serena bit her lip, then said with dignity, 'If you must know, I was thinking that you . . . that you'd sent me to . . . to Coventry.'

'My dear child!' Sean was laughing at her openly now. 'Why on earth would I do that?'

'You weren't very nice to me yesterday morning,' she said stiffly. 'I appreciate all the trouble I put you to, but I did apologise and try to explain, so . . .'

'And I accepted all your apologies and explanations,' he broke in wryly. 'If I wasn't . . . very nice to you in the process, it was simply because I had other things on my mind. How are you? Up to getting on a horse?'

'But . . . I'm fine,' Serena said confusedly.

'The last time you told me that it wasn't exactly true,' he drawled.

'Well, I am now,' she retorted. 'I'm not at all stiff any more and I've fallen off horses enough times not to have to get straight back on—if that's what you've got in mind. Well, more or less straight back on . . .'

He overrode her. 'It's not quite what I had in mind, so you can save your breath—and your indignation. Just get changed into riding gear with a swimming costume underneath, bring a towel and meet me at the front gate in five minutes.' He turned on his heel and strode away.

Serena blinked, opened her mouth to protest but changed her mind. He was gone anyway.

Her expression was shuttered, however, as she arrived at the front gate six minutes later, even though she was rather breathless.

There were two horses tethered to the fence and Sean was leaning back against it with his arms folded. One of the horses was his tall black gelding, but it was the other that caused Serena to forget her resolve to be cool and unforthcoming. 'Oh, isn't she lovely!' she said involuntarily of the glossy brown mare with gentle, intelligent eyes. 'Where did she come from?' She stroked the velvety nose.

'She's been here all the time but on a different part of the property. So you approve?'

'Mmm.' Serena wasn't really listening as she smoothed the mare's forelock, but Sean's next words snapped her to attention.

'Good. She's yours.'

Serena pulled her hand away as if burnt. 'Mine! H-how can she be mine?' she stammered, her violet eyes wide with bewilderment.

He grinned and said lazily, 'Quite simple. She's reserved for your exclusive use while you stay with us so that you won't have to put up with . . . pigheaded, obstinate nags with nothing in their heads but thoughts of tucker. You'll have to look after her yourself, though. Care to try her?'

It was only after they'd been for a glorious gallop and were walking their horses side by side that Serena was able to express herself adequately. 'I feel terrible now.'

Sean glanced at her wryly. 'Oh?'

'For thinking such . . . negative thoughts about you earlier,' she explained.

'Oh.' His lips twisted. 'That. Don't worry about it, I'm . . . quite used to it now.'

'That only makes me feel even *worse* . . .'

'Dear me,' he observed, 'I did have something else in mind this morning, something designed to make you feel even *better,* but if all I'm going to achieve is this . . .' He shrugged.

Serena eyed him suspiciously. 'Now you're teasing me.'

'Perish the thought,' he murmured.

'What could make me feel even better than this?' She patted the mare's neck. 'What's her name, by the way?'

'Sally. Have you ever seen a real billabong? With coolibah trees?'

'No,' Serena said slowly. She looked around. They were walking through a cypress forest with the vista of open grassland beyond—Mitchell and Flinders grasses which made excellent grazing.

'Then I'll show you some.' Sean flicked his horse into a canter and she followed suit until, after about fifteen minutes, they came to a series of discontinuous waterholes, full now and teeming with birdlife on the ground and in the surrounding coolibahs—sprawling, gnarled old eucalypts with massive trunks and narrow leaves.

Serena was enchanted into a wondering silence until finally she said in awed voice, 'I've never seen anything like it.'

'Like to have a swim? This one is pretty deep. It could be cold, but that should help your bruises.'

They dismounted and tied their horses up, and Sean gave them each a drink out of his wide-brimmed hat. Then he unhooked a saddlebag and a billycan without which no self-respecting stockman travels, set up a tripod and made a small fire beneath it. He filled the billy with water and lit the fire, took a rolled-up groundsheet off his horse and spread it out, and said, 'Right, by the time we've had our swim that should be boiling. Bet I beat you in!'

The water, although it looked a bit like milky tea, was marvellous—after the initial plunge which all but took Serena's breath away.

'I thought the water out here sometimes came up b-b-boiling!'

'This didn't come up from an artesian bore, it came down from heaven—and the nights are getting cold.'

'You're not wrong! I hope my bruises appreciate what I'm doing for them.'

He laughed. And when they climbed out, he made her stand still while he inspected her person clad in her blue one-piece costume.

'Mmm,' he said, touching one livid patch on her thigh and another on her arm, 'you came down on your side, by the look of it. Lucky you didn't break anything. Here,' he handed her her towel, 'dry off while I make the tea.'

'Yes, Dad,' she said with an impish grin.

'Just like to check on all my responsibilities,' he replied imperturbably. 'How does the idea of some fresh damper to go with your tea sound?'

'Scrumptious!' she said with a giggle.

They sat in the dappled sunlight and drank

strong, sweet tea, and he told her about the different kinds of birds that frequented these waterholes and creeks.

'In good seasons you even see pelicans.'

'Pelicans!'

'Yep. There are also brolas and—but you know about the Major Mitchell cockatoos.'

'I learned about them at school, although I still haven't seen any. But they're pink and white, aren't they?'

'Yes, and getting a bit rarer, unfortunately. More damper?'

'Thanks—Sean, we should have brought the twins!'

'I reckoned you deserved a break from them. Even the most devoted, untiring governess needs a break.'

'And a marvellous treat.' Serena breathed deeply as she looked around. 'I don't know what to say—except thank you.'

Sean was sitting cross-legged on the ground in a pair of maroon bathers, squinting through his damp hair which he hadn't bothered to dry, and a ghost of a smile touched his lips as he said quizzically, 'You're a . . . strange child in some ways, you know.'

Serena hesitated, fiddled with her last bit of damper, then said, 'Sometimes I wish you'd treat me like a woman.'

There was a moment's clear, piercing silence until he said, 'The one time I did you appeared to be oddly bewildered and then extremely cross with me.'

Serena's lips parted, then she rushed into speech,

'Do you mean . . . oh, I didn't mean like *that*. Not . . . I mean, I didn't want you to kiss me or anything like that.' Her cheeks grew hot and she tried to speak further, but her words got impossibly jumbled.

'Treat you like an adult, then. Is that what you meant?' he supplied.

'Oh, yes!' Serena stared at him, flooded with relief, then she became agitated again. 'Please don't think I'm criticising this marvellous treat—I mean, it's not childish to enjoy something like this, is it? I . . .' She broke off.

'Perhaps not,' he mused. 'Such spontaneous delight at really very simple things is—well, different, though.'

'Do you mean—different from the kind of women you know?' Serena forgot her agitation and was suddenly deeply interested. 'Do you know very many?'

Sean shot her a glinting, amused look. 'Enough.'

'Well, I don't want to pry, but I've wondered about that,' she said seriously. 'When I first met you I thought there might be lots—not all at the same time, naturally,' she hastened to assure him.

'Thank you,' he drawled.

'Or at least, one serious one,' she continued. 'But there's . . . no one.' A perplexed frown wrinkled her brow.

'How do you know that?' he countered.

'If she was serious—I mean, if you were seriously in love, surely you'd talk about her, write to her . . . *be* with her. Or is it a case of unrequited love?' she asked him anxiously.

Sean stared at her in a totally deadpan way for

nearly a full minute, then he said softly and rather ruefully, 'My dear Serena, I knew I was taking on the unknown when I took you on, but I didn't even realise a fraction of it.'

Serena blushed. 'I'm sorry . . .'

'Now don't go all prim on me,' he commanded.

'Then you're not offended?' she asked uncertainly.

He grinned suddenly. 'I'm not quite sure. I take it you don't approve of me having no one—if that's the case?'

Serena shrugged. 'It seems a bit of a waste. You've got an awful lot going for you and if you plan to have children . . . I think it's a mistake to wait too long. Not that I know exactly how old you are . . .'

'I'm thirty-two,' he told her politely. 'Old enough to have one foot in the grave at least.'

'Now you *are* teasing me,' she said with a chuckle. 'Sorry, I didn't mean to make it sound like that.'

'I'm relieved,' he commented, but as she continued to eye him with considerable, expectant interest, he added wryly, 'I think I'll reserve the right to maintain my privacy on the matter of my love life, dear Miss Abigail. I . . . er . . . prefer it that way, and anyway, that's a right you vigorously champion when it comes to *your* love life.'

'What love life?' Serena enquired.

'You don't have any?'

'Not *love*,' she said with unmistakable bitterness. Then she coloured and looked away.

'I suppose it's no good asking you to elaborate,' he said quietly after a time.

'No,' she whispered, then deliberately brightened

her voice and expression. 'You *haven't* asked me how I got on with Richard!'

'Well, go on, I'm agog,' he said, but drily.

She told him what had passed between her and Richard.

'I . . . see,' he said slowly. 'And do you think you convinced him?'

Serena grimaced. 'With Richard it's hard to tell, but I think having at least . . . sort of voiced it, he could feel less pressured about it. Is . . .' She stopped, then started again, 'Is their mother aware of these problems?'

'Delvene has a singularly one-track mind,' Sean said, so coldly that Serena shivered inwardly. 'And I think the time might have come to . . . enlighten her about it.'

'You'd have to be very careful how you did that, wouldn't you?' she said, wide-eyed and a little apprehensively. 'I mean, if the twins thought you two were . . . fighting or something like that, it could upset them more.'

'That's exactly why *she* thinks she has me over a barrel.' He looked away into the sunlight, his eyes narrowed and his mouth suddenly hard and grim.

'Oh, dear,' Serena said a little helplessly. 'In a way I'm sorry I mentioned it, but you did tell me . . '

'Of course you had to tell me,' he said impatiently.

'Well, that's what I thought, but I could have waited and not spoiled this lovely morning,' she said sadly.

'Serena . . .' He looked at her exasperatedly, then

relaxed suddenly. 'All right, we won't spoil your lovely morning. We'll take our time riding back, I'll show you some more wondrous things—and we have a week before Delvene descends on us, so we might as well make the best of it. Don't worry,' he added to her look of doubt, 'I won't do anything to upset the twins.'

During that week, Serena realised several things. That she really felt part of the family, for one thing, that she was enjoying life as she hadn't for a long time for another, but there was also something that puzzled her in that peaceful—even Richard desisted from any mischief—week. She felt as if she was on the brink of something, as if she was holding her breath, metaphorically speaking. She tried to probe the cause of this nameless sort of expectation that tripped her up while she was doing the most mundane things, such as helping Mrs Denby on her baking day or playing with the kitten the twins had found and presented her with—to atone for Richard's sins, she suspected.

'But where did you find it?' she asked laughingly as the black and white ball of fluff exploded out of the shoebox they had it captive in, spitting furiously and showing all its spiky teeth and small pink tongue.

'In the stables,' Cameron said offhandedly.

Sean came upon the three of them sitting cross-legged on the floor in the twins' bedroom doing a jig-saw puzzle before bed, with the kitten curled up in Serena's lap.

'What's this?' he enquired.

'We found it in the feed shed, Sean,' Richard said glibly.

'I have explained to you about how the place could get overrun, haven't I, by cats?' Sean remarked.

'This is a boy,' Cameron pointed out, then said pleadingly, 'And you should see how it loves Serena! All it wants to do is scratch us.'

'Does Serena love *it*?'

'She talks baby talk to it and she's fixed up a special basket for it in her bedroom and she feeds it every three hours with a dropper because it's so little—I reckon so.' This was Richard's contribution.

'And what does she call it?' Sean asked resignedly.

'Oh dear—have I done the wrong thing?' Serena followed the course of the conversation with her lips parted. 'I thought I might train it to keep my bed free of mice and frogs. If the need should ever arise again,' she added hastily.

'Do I take it you're siding with Richard and Cameron, Serena?''

Serena smiled up at him engagingly and, by way of reply, lifted the cat which was barely larger than her palm for him to see. 'I thought I might call him Rupert—only if you'll allow him to stay, of course.'

'Rupert,' Sean said ironically.

'I know it's a rather pretentious name for such a little cat, but I thought it might encourage him to grow to bigger and better things.'

'If that's not blackmail I don't know what is,' Sean observed but with his lips twitching. 'Very well, it can stay, but I refuse to call it Rupert until I see some justification for it.'

The twins beseiged him delightedly—and Serena, watching her charges with their tall uncle, experienced another of those breathless attacks.

That night in bed, however, she found herself thinking that it was going to be awfully hard to leave Rosewood.

Then it was D-Day, as she had come to call it in her mind.

The day Delvene was due. Bill had gone down to Sydney to pick her up, and it seemed to Serena as if everyone was thoroughly over-excited or tense—except Sean.

But when the appointed hour came and they waited in the shade of the shed for the plane, saw it land and saw its passenger alight, Serena realised that none of her mental pictures of the twins' mother, which had suffered somewhat from the thought that she had to be rather heartless to say the least, did Delvene justice.

She *was* beautiful. Tall, with streaky ash-blonde hair, a superb carriage and the ability to turn a pair of blue jea s and a white blouse into a couturier outfit.

As she jumped down, she tossed her head, took a deep appreciative breath, and Serena caught herself thinking another of those unexpected thoughts—that this would be the type of blended sophistication and beauty that would appeal to Sean . . .

Then the twins were dragging their mother towards her and Delvene was saying breathlessly, 'Hello, Serena! I've been looking forward to meeting you!' And her clear green eyes were warm and very friendly.

It was impossible not to smile back.

Getting ready for bed that night, Serena found herself chewing her lip thoughtfully and trying to set things straight in her mind. Such as—had Delvene been maligned by both Sean and Mrs Denby? Could anyone as warm and friendly be as heartless as they thought she was? Had they allowed their natural antagonism over the divorce of two ill-suited people to affect their judgement?

'Well, it is a bit unnatural to leave her children here, but she did explain that to me,' she murmured to herself, and cast her mind back over the conversation she had had with Delvene as she was getting ready for dinner . . .

She was standing in her ivory silk slip when there came a light tap on her door.

'Only me,' she heard Delvene say. 'May I come in?'

'Um . . . yes!' Serena looked around for her dress, but it was still hanging in the wardrobe as Delvene slipped into the room.

'Oh, sorry!'

'No, it's all right—is there something I can do for you?'

'I just came in for a chat,' Delvene said with a smile. 'Bill has the boys under control, so we might get some peace and quiet for a few minutes——You know,' she stopped and studied Serena, 'you're just gorgeous!'

Serena blushed. 'Th-thank you,' she stammered, 'but . . .'

'No, you are,' Delvene said admiringly.

'Well, to be honest, I thought you were . . . I was even wondering how I could learn to be so . . . elegant and sophisticated . . .'

'Oh, God,' Delvene said ruefully, at the same time casting herself down into the armchair, 'you make me feel about a hundred!'

'I didn't mean that, it's a beautifully casual sort of . . . elegance too.'

'All the same, it'd be nice to be . . . eighteen? Yes, eighteen again and so fresh and unspoilt—which brings me to what I . . . really came to see you about.' Delvene's expression changed, sobered. 'You must wonder about this set-up, Serena?'

'I . . . well,' Serena said awkwardly, 'Sean has . . .'

'I'm sure he has. I thought I might give you my version, though. Would you mind?' Delvene's green eyes were direct and just a little challenging.

'I . . .' Serena hesitated.

'I wouldn't expect you to be disloyal to Sean—or anything like that.'

Serena bit her lip, then she said quietly, 'I'm very much in Sean's debt, one way or another, so . . .' she stopped as Delvene's eyes widened slightly, 'it . . . but you are their mother.'

'Thank you. Unfortunately, I'm not one of those mothers who can devote their lives to their children. I have a career and it's a very demanding one, but it's also the one thing I'm *good* at, and although I know Sean would always provide for the twins, financially as well as otherwise, I don't want that, and I also have myself to provide for. Don't get me wrong! It's not that I'm not grateful to Sean and it's not that I don't agree that this is a much better life-style for them, I do, and as you can see, I've taken advantage of that for *their* sakes, but I don't want to be totally beholden. Can you understand that, Serena?'

Serena hesitated. 'I can,' she said slowly.

'But you have some reservations?' Delvene queried.

'I think it might be a bit hard for *them* to under-stand . . .'

'Ah! Go on,' Delvene invited intently.

'Well, now they're older and can read and write, why don't you write them letters? And instead of you only coming up to see them, perhaps they could come down and see you occasionally. It . . . might make them feel more a part of your life.'

'Which *you* feel . . . they lack?'

'Just a little,' Serena said cautiously. 'But perhaps you ought to talk to Sean about that, he knows them so well—oh, there goes the dinner bell!'

'Saved by the bell?' Delvene asked, but when Serena coloured, she smiled warmly. 'Sorry—I don't know what Sean has told you about me, but I guess it's obvious we have our disagreements from time to time.' She got up and moved slowly about the room with that fluid dancer's walk, idly touching and examining things such as Serena's monogrammed silver-backed hairbrush and mirror, her beautifully embroidered velvet nightgown case and the exquisite Royal Doulton china basket of flowers on her bedside table.

When she straightened, her eyes were thoughtful and faintly speculative and she said, 'What made you take a job like this, Serena?'

Serena considered and decided she could answer honestly. 'I always wanted to see this part of the world. I'm . . . rather wrapped up in it.'

Delvene looked rueful. 'Sean must think you've dropped from heaven! We thought that was going to be a major problem—finding someone who'd *like* living out here. I should imagine he—we, that is—are more in your debt than the other way around!'

'I don't know about that,' Serena said with a faint smile.

'Anyway,' Delvene continued warmly, 'I'd like to thank you very much for taking such good care of Richard and Cameron—they're certainly *wrapped up* in you! And I'll definitely be taking your advice.'

'Er . . . well,' Serena started to say, unable not to wonder what Sean would think of her presuming to offer such advice, 'I . . .'

'Don't worry,' Delvene said humorously, 'I'll check it out with him first—see you at dinner!'

And she was gone, leaving Serena to stand in the middle of her bedroom, not entirely reassured, but after a moment or two, she shrugged and grimaced and reached for her slim, dusky pink linen dress.

All the same, she thought, as she got into bed later that night, having checked on Rupert first, I like her, and she must have been left in a rather awkward situation, and when he's *with* her, Sean doesn't seem to mind her either. Even Denny manages to be pleasant. They can't be acting entirely, can they?

CHAPTER FIVE

DELVENE stayed at Rosewood for four days, during which time a holiday from school was declared, much to Richard and Cameron's amazement. They even had the picnic so dear to Richard's heart, a barbecue one evening, and throughout the four days no one would have guessed there were any tensions at work. At least, had she not accidentally been privy to a private conversation between Delvene and Sean, Serena would have assumed that they had sorted out their differences.

It was the night before Delvene was due to leave that she got up quite late to heat up some milk for Rupert—it was cold and he was restless and crying rather piteously. She thought some warm milk in his tummy might settle him. Then it dawned on her, as she padded noiselessly into the kitchen, that in the dead quiet of the night she could clearly hear a conversation taking place in the study which opened on to the veranda on the other side of the kitchen. She hesitated, conscious of not wishing to eavesdrop, but then realised they were discussing her, and for the life of her was unable to beat a hasty retreat.

'She's an unusual child, Serena is,' Delvene was saying.

'Is that why you're wandering around in the middle of the night? To discuss Serena?' Sean enquired.

'Not really—I couldn't sleep, and anyway, there are some things we *should* discuss. Why are you working so late, by the way?'

'I'm off to Brisbane tomorrow,' Sean said briefly.

'Oh—well, she is an unusual child, isn't she? Where did you find her?'

'I advertised. Incidentally, she'd be cut to the quick to know you thought of her as a child.'

Serena grimaced as Delvene laughed softly and said, 'My apologies to Serena. She,' Delvene paused, 'for some reason seems to think she's indebted to you.'

'Does she? I can't imagine why,' drawled Sean. 'If anything it's the other way around.'

'That's what I would have thought. Richard and Cameron are quite taken with her.'

There was a short silence, then Sean said, 'What brought that up?'

'What up?'

'Her imagined indebtedness to me.' Sean sounded dry.

'We were discussing the twins, actually,' Delvene replied. 'She was giving me the benefit of her advice— which I intend to take, I must warn you, Sean.'

Serena held her breath.

'Do enlighten me,' Sean invited, sounding even drier.

'She thinks I should play a much greater part in their lives—she thinks I should make them feel more part of *my* life. Little does she know how you've opposed me on that in the past, Sean, nor did I enlighten her, but . . .'

Sean cut in, 'All I ever opposed was your carting them around from pillar to post or abandoning them to a nanny—which was why you left them here with Andrew in the first place,' he said harshly. 'It was also his expressed wish that they should be able to grow up here, or had you forgotten?'

'Sean,' Delvene said almost pleadingly, 'what happened between me and Andrew was . . . well, it was one of those things! When are you going to stop punishing me for it?'

Serena heard the sound of a chair being scraped back and then Sean's voice came from much closer, making her start a little. 'Punishing you?' he said sardonically.

'You know what I mean,' Delvene said softly.

'Delvene, if you mean what I think you mean, you're wasting your time. And Richard and Cameron stay here.'

'I could go to court,' said Delvene after a time in a strained voice.

'You could, but you won't. This arrangement suits you too well—and for God's sake, don't go raving on about this to Serena or trying to touch her heartstrings,' said Sean as if irritated beyond words. 'Heaven knows what problems that could lead to!'

'I won't—of course I won't—but I don't think I understand what you mean.'

'You don't know Serena as well as I do, that's all,' Sean said shortly.

'What . . . what if I were to tell you I was . . . thinking of getting married again? What then, Sean?'

'Are you?' He sounded derisive. 'Or is this just another . . .'

A second chair scraped back as Delvene hissed, 'I hate you sometimes, Sean Wentworth!'

But he only laughed in a way that made Serena shiver curiously.

There was another silence and Serena found she could picture Sean and Delvene clearly in her mind's eye. Sean would be at his ease but with that mocking glint in his eye as he surveyed Delvene, whereas she would be radiating hostility, her beautiful, lithe body tense, her magnificent green eyes flashing with anger and frustration. *I* could have told you, Serena thought a little sadly, that it's almost impossible to get the better of Sean Wentworth, but then I'm surprised you didn't know.

'All the same, I'm going to take Serena's advice,' Delvene said tautly then. 'I'm not quite the heartless bitch you take me for.'

'I'm agog,' drawled Sean. 'Which bit of Serena's advice—I presume it was quite extensive?'

Serena bit her lip.

'That they visit *me* occasionally—visit being the operative word, dear Sean,' Delvene emphasised, 'before you get the wrong idea. I even thought I might take them back with me tomorrow for a couple of days. Cross my heart and hope to die, I will not abscond with them nor endanger their morals, and . . .'

But Sean interrupted her. 'Great minds do think alike,' he murmured. 'I was going to suggest something like that myself.'

If Delvene was momentarily stunned, Serena felt her chest muscles relax with relief.

'Then you don't mind?' It was as if Delvene couldn't believe her ears.

'I'm not in the habit of suggesting things I do mind —besides, you may not have noticed this, but Richard has lately . . .'

It was at this point that Serena realised she had no excuse—if she'd ever had a legitimate one—for eavesdropping any further. So she made her way hastily and silently back to her bedroom, feeling guilty but relieved. Then she realised she'd forgotten about Rupert's milk, but he had curled himself up into a tight little ball and was sound asleep.

So she got back into bed—and discovered that her heartstrings were touched, and wondered why. Because Sean couldn't forgive his ex-sister-in-law for running away from his brother? Well, she mused, don't forget you're an outsider. It's always easier for an outsider to see things . . . I mean, if he'd been my brother I might find it hard to forgive, too. But she's not a bad person, I don't think.

The next morning brought scenes of great excitement.

'Serena, Serena—guess what?'

'What?' She feigned surprise as well as she could.

'We're going to Sydney with Mum today . . .' Richard announced.

'To stay with her till the end of the week!' Cameron added wonderingly. 'Denny's coming too. To look after us when Mum has rehearsals—and to take us to the dentist.' His expression fell momentarily, but it was obvious that even the prospect of a visit to the dentist would not be allowed to cloud his joy for long.

'Hey, that's fabulous!' Serena said warmly, but she was actually discreetly searching Richard's expression for a clue to the true state of his feelings. Which was why it didn't occur to her immediately that perhaps it ought to be her job to look after them while their mother was in rehearsal.

Then Delvene said, 'I did suggest to Sean that you come down, Serena, but he's commanded Denny to the task, so Denny it will be!'

'I . . . oh,' Serena said slowly, and thought, I wonder why? Perhaps he thinks I'll be too easily led astray away from the wilds of Rosewood? I bet that's it, she thought indignantly, but took care not to allow her expression to betray her feelings. There was no point anyway, the object of her indignation, one Sean Wentworth, was, as usual, not at breakfast.

But it was Denny herself who caused Serena to wonder if she was maligning Sean for once, when she said, 'I'm really overdue for a visit to the dentist myself. I have a tooth which I suspect needs filling. Sean thought you might not mind taking over the house for me, Serena?'

'Oh. No, of course not!'

'I thought not,' said Denny. 'Well, I guess we should get this show on the road! Bill reckons we'll leave at midday. Sean was going to Brisbane himself today, Serena, but he's cancelled it. I don't think he's expecting any visitors over the next few days, but you never know, so I'll run through some menus with you just in case. And should you get inundated, by any chance, Susie Jones will come up to help you.' Susie Jones was the seventeen-year-old daughter of the station blacksmith. 'Then we've got to pack.'

By midday, Serena was feeling quite breathless as she and Sean waved the plane off. Then, almost immediately, she experienced a feeling of anticlimax.

'Well,' she said to Sean, 'I mean . . . well.'

'Well what?' he queried with a faint smile.

'I don't really know—I feel at a bit of a loose end.'

'You could . . . relax,' he suggested.

'I'm not very good at that—I mean, doing nothing.'

'There is a difference between relaxing and doing nothing,' he said wryly. 'You could read, write letters . . . although you don't do much of that, do you?'

'Not a lot,' Serena agreed, then added hastily, 'It's just that I didn't expect to be *able* to relax, I think. I mean, this all came up rather out of the blue, didn't it?'

'It was also your idea, I'm told.'

'Well,' Serena said cautiously, 'Delvene did ask me and . . . you don't mind, do you?'

Sean studied her meditatively for a moment. Then he said almost abruptly, 'What did you think of her?'

'Delvene? I . . .' Serena hesitated, 'she . . . I think she's one of those gifted kind of people whose family has to trail along in the wake, sort of. But I also think she *does* care for the twins and now that they can feel more a part of her life, they'll probably make the necessary adjustments. Children do.'

Sean was silent for so long and his expression was so enigmatic, a worried frown touched Serena's brow.

He observed this and his lips twisted wryly as he murmured, 'Out of the mouths of babes—that was meant to be a compliment, incidentally. Hop in,' he added, gesturing to the Land Rover they had all come down to the airstrip in, 'I'll give you a lift back to the house, where you'll have to start practising the art of relaxing.'

'What will you be doing?' Serena enquired as they bounced along the track.

'I'm going to see a bore they're having trouble with—I should be back by about four-thirty. Bill will be back around five. Don't go to a lot of trouble for dinner for just the three of us. Out you get,' Sean commanded as the Land Rover slid to a dusty halt outside the garden gate.

Serena glanced at him speculatively.

'What?' he asked.

'Nothing . . .'

'No, I'm not going to take you with me, Serena, if that's what you have in mind,' he said drily.

'I just thought . . . I've never seen a bore working.'

'There's not a lot to see. It'll also be a hot, dusty drive.'

'I don't mind that!'

'Serena,' he said deliberately, 'no.'

'Have I done something wrong?' she enquired.

Sean said impatiently, 'Of course not!'

'Then why . . .'

'All right, I'll explain fully.' He eyed her impatiently. 'This bore is situated at a camp. There are three resident bore workers at the camp and it's their job to check and maintain all the bores in that area. They live out there a month on and a week off, with only one weekly trip into headquarters. Consequently they're rather starved for the sight of the human female.'

'Oh.' Serena coloured. 'I . . .'

'It would be extremely difficult for them to concentrate on repairing this bore with . . . particularly an example of the species like you around and . . .'

'I'm going, I'm going,' muttered Serena, and fled the Land Rover. Sean drove off at speed.

'I can't *help* being a female of the species!' Serena shouted at the departing Land Rover with more spirit. 'And for your information, Sean Wentworth, all it's ever brought me is a whole lot of trouble, which is extremely *unfair,* I think, if you must know!'

In the end, her afternoon passed quite peacefully. She had a light lunch and made preparations for dinner. Then she found a book, changed into her swimming costume and took a towel to a lovely green patch of lawn beside the creeper-covered tank stands, where she passed the time pleasantly, sunbathing and reading.

Good as his word, Sean brought the Land Rover back at four-thirty, but he went straight into the shower. Serena gathered up her things and went to change herself, slipping into a pair of jeans and a fuchsia pink jumper. She brushed her hair and plaited it into one thick rope that fell over her shoulder. Then, after a cursory glance at herself in the mirror, she removed to the kitchen to start dinner. But a strange birdcall distracted her and she went out on to the veranda to see if she could see the bird, to no avail, and instead saw the Land Rover Bill used, driving up the track.

'That was a quick trip,' she murmured to herself, then, as the Land Rover stopped and both front doors opened, she grimaced, for it was obvious Bill had brought a visitor who, no doubt, she would have to feed as well. Her mind flew over the meal she had prepared and its stretchability—a term Denny had coined from frequently being placed thus.

It was at this point that she realised there was something vaguely familiar about Bill's visitor. Then her

eyes narrowed and she gasped and whispered, 'No
. . . Oh, no!' and turned to run inside.

Unfortunately, as she shot around a corner, she
cannoned into Sean.

'Whoa there!' he murmured, putting out a hand
to steady her. 'Where's the fire?'

'Take your hands off me!' she hissed at him. 'You
. . . *traitor!* How *could* you?' And she raised her hand.

He caught it and said grimly, 'Don't, Serena.
Unless you want your face slapped back. And would
you mind telling me what you're babbling on
about?' He held her wrist in an iron grip.

'I *trusted* you!' she stormed at him. 'But you not
only had to probe and pry around, you've even
flown him up here! Well, I told him and I told *her*
and I'm telling you now, I'd rather die than marry
him. Do you understand?' Her voice rose
hysterically.

'I understand nothing,' Sean said through his
teeth. 'But if you don't calm down I will slap you,'
he warned. 'Come in here,' he added brusquely,
and shouldered open the study door.

He bundled her into the room and turned back to
the door as Bill tapped on it.

'Perhaps you can explain this to me, Bill,' he said
impatiently.

Bill frowned as he took in Serena's distraught
appearance. 'Someone here to see Serena,' he said.
'That what you mean?'

'Apparently,' Sean said shortly. 'How did he get
here?'

'Got dropped off from the milk run, far as I can tell.
Found him down at the store making enquiries, so I

ferried him up here.'

Serena shivered. 'I don't want to see him,' she whispered fearfully, her eyes huge.

Sean stared at her with narrowed eyes, then he said peremptorily to Bill, 'Will you tell—whoever this is, that Serena is indisposed at the moment. Tell him what you like, but keep . . . give him a drink or something, but keep him away until I sort this out.'

Bill nodded and went out, closing the door, while Sean crossed to a cocktail cabinet and splashed some brandy into a glass.

'Drink this.' He offered the glass to Serena, then closed his eyes briefly in irritation as she gulped at the liquid. 'Don't gulp it, sip it,' he commanded.

She did as she was bid and some colour crept into her cheeks.

'Now,' he pulled a chair up opposite her and sat down astride it, 'suppose you tell me what this is all about.'

'You mean . . . you don't know who Ralph is? But how did he find me, then?'

Sean shrugged. 'Search me.' He took the empty glass from her and twisted round to put it down on the desk behind him. 'Who is this . . . er . . . Ralph?'

Serena hesitated miserably.

'Serena,' Sean said softly but coldly, 'I'm getting a little tired of repeating myself, but for the record, I'll say again—I know nothing. However, I don't intend to remain in this fog of ignorance where you're concerned any longer. Our bargain is now ended. And if you expect me to . . . save you from this Ralph character, which seems to me to be the case—or am I wrong?'

Serena shivered. 'No.'

'Then you'd better tell me the truth, the whole truth and nothing but, starting now,' he ordered.

She swallowed and licked her lips. 'It's not easy,' she said helplessly.

'I never imagined it was. Why don't you try for some sort of chronological order?'

She thought for a moment, then said haltingly, 'It . . . all began when my mother died. I was fourteen. My father was just bereft, they'd been very close. Then, right out of the blue, to me anyway, he got married again! I couldn't believe it. She, my stepmother, was younger than he was, quite a bit, and . . . and if you must know, I hated her!' she said passionately.

'That doesn't altogether surprise me,' Sean murmured with a grin tugging at his lips. 'It comes rather easily to you—this ability to hate people. As I should know,' he added with an ironic look, then his eyes softened briefly. 'All right, I can understand how you felt. What happened then?'

Serena's lips quivered. 'He died suddenly of a heart attack.' She wiped away a solitary tear. 'It . . . then I found out he'd known he had heart problems and he'd made a will appointing her as my guardian and trustee in case of such an eventuality.'

There was a small silence during which Sean's eyes sharpened. 'I see,' he said at last. 'Where does this Ralph come into it all?'

'He . . . he's her brother,' Serena said tightly. 'He came to live with us after my father died. You see, in the will, my father left her our Melbourne house and a small income, but all the rest of it, including the sheep station, he left to me, but . . . it was all left in trust until I was twenty-one or until I married, whichever came first.'

'Ah,' Sean said softly, 'I begin to see the light. A curious will to leave, though,' he commented.

'He was besotted,' Serena said bitterly. 'Maybe because he was so lonely, but he never realised she was after his money. I'm sure she persuaded him to insert that clause and I suppose it's just lucky she didn't manage to get him to leave it all to her outright.'

'If it's as you say, she might have realised you'd have every hope of fighting it. Go on.'

'Well, for a while it wasn't so bad. I was at boarding school—at least that hadn't changed—and during the holidays, they used to . . . almost go out of their way to see that I had a good time. You know, shows, picnics, days at the beach, lovely clothes . . .' She stopped. 'I even began to think she wasn't so bad after all, and Ralph wasn't there much . . . but after I turned seventeen I began to notice that he used to look at me a lot. I didn't like it.'

'What else did he do?' asked Sean after a moment.

'Well,' Serena hesitated, 'then I began to notice that he was always trying to touch me. It . . . it gave me the creeps.' She shuddered.

'Serena,' Sean said, 'are you trying to tell me your stepmother planned to marry you off to her brother? To get their hands on your inheritance?'

'Y-yes,' she stammered. 'Once I left school, it really came clear to me what was going on. I wanted to travel and do things I'd been dreaming about for years, but they wouldn't let me. They wouldn't let me out of their sight! And all the time he was watching me and . . . and . . .'

'All right,' said Sean with a sort of rough concern.

'Don't torment yourself. And she held the purse-strings, of course,' he added almost to himself. 'No other relatives to turn to, I gather?'

'No,' Serena said sadly. 'And one day, I just couldn't bear it any longer, so . . .'

'So you ran away.'

'It was the only thing I could do . . . well,' she amended tautly, 'the other option didn't appeal to me.'

'Other option?'

'Finding someone else to marry me—I mean, just so that I could get my hands on what was rightfully mine.'

'I see,' Sean said gravely, although his eyes were amused. 'That could have been a little dangerous, too.'

Serena grimaced. 'It wasn't really an option—for one thing I didn't know anyone, they saw to that, and for another, Ralph's really turned me off that sort of thing anyway. He . . . he makes me feel sick.'

'That doesn't mean every man you meet will have the same effect on you,' he commented, then frowned. 'If that's the case, though, working at the Pelican Club must have been rather unpleasant.'

'It was,' Serena agreed gloomily. 'When you're hungry it's surprising what you can put up with, though. But I wasn't a great success there. I . . . I got fired the day after you rescued me from that awful bike rider—I didn't tell you that,' she added a shade nervously.

'I already knew—why didn't you apply for the dole?'

Serena sighed. 'I was afraid if I did, they might be able to trace me through it. I used my mother's maiden name to get the job at the club.'

'I see,' Sean said.

'Do . . . do you believe me?' Serena asked tremulously.

'Strangely enough, I do. It's about the only explanation that seems to fit—now I know you better,' he said quizzically. 'Although why you couldn't have told me all this sooner, I fail to see,' he added.

'I didn't know *you* very well, did I?' she offered. 'I mean, I wasn't to know you wouldn't turn out like Ralph, so I thought it was best to keep it to myself.'

A curious glint came into Sean's eyes as he regarded her steadily until she started to colour, then she rushed into speech. 'Of course, it wasn't long before I started to realise you weren't like that at all . . .'

'How kind of you,' he murmured.

'But I still didn't know whether you mightn't think it your duty to hand me back,' she whispered, and put out a trembling hand to touch his. 'You won't, will you . . .?'

'I . . .' he took her hand in his and gazed down at it, 'Serena . . .'

But Serena sat up with a gasp, her eyes brightening. 'I've just thought of something! Sean—I'd be the last person you'd ever marry, wouldn't I?'

He stared at her, his eyes narrowing.

'I mean, I'm not your type, am I, and I'm miles too young for you, and anyway, I don't . . . well, I don't turn you on, do I?'

'Serena . . .'

But Serena was not to be interrupted. 'The other thing is, you wouldn't be interested in my inheritance, would you? You seem to have more than enough of your own, don't you?'

'Serena, what the hell is this leading up to?'

'Would . . . Sean,' Serena took a deep breath, 'would you consider marrying me?'

He swore, and she winced but pressed on. 'I only mean a marriage of convenience . . . just for as long as it takes to *get* my inheritance. Nobody need even know about it . . . nobody here. We could carry on as we have . . .'

'Serena,' Sean broke in, in a voice that made her pale a little, 'no.'

'Sean . . .'

'No.'

She was white to the lips now. 'But I don't know what else to do,' she whispered pleadingly. 'It's over two years until I'm twenty-one, and that's a long time to be running away and living on my wits . . .'

'Serena, he can't carry you kicking and screaming to the altar . . .'

'You don't know what he's like! Anyway, I've got this horrible feeling he might not . . . wait until he gets me to the altar, if he gets his hands on me again. I'm . . . perhaps because you're a man, you don't understand what it's like, but he not only revolts me and . . . makes me feel sick, he . . . *frightens* me so much. Even to think he's in the same house . . .' She stopped and buried her face in her hands.

'Serena,' Sean said at last in a different voice, 'look at me.'

She did, reluctantly, her eyes shadowed with desperation and with silent tears streaming down her face.

He frowned and reached out a hand to touch her wet cheek. 'Tell me something—would you be happy to stay here with us until you're twenty-one?'

'Of course I would,' she said desolately. 'I love it

here and I love my job, but . . .'

'Are you quite sure?'

'Yes, but . . .'

'Then dry your tears, because I'm going to get this Ralph in here . . . and make some things very clear to the bastard.'

'Why don't you sit down, Mr Taylor,' Sean said coolly.

Ralph Taylor was as tall as Sean, but that was about the only point of resemblance between them other than that they were about the same age. But whereas Sean carried not a spare ounce of flesh on his tall, lithe, well-proportioned body, Ralph's outline was blurred from years of good living and little exercise.

Serena tore her gaze from his fleshy lips, and suppressed a shudder.

Sean indicated a chair and Ralph sat, but with his muddy brown eyes alert as if he was trying to sense the air.

'I believe you've come to see Serena,' said Sean.

Ralph smiled and his gaze flickered over Serena. 'Not only that, but I can't tell you how relieved we are to have found her!' he said silkily.

'When you say we, does that mean you and your sister?'

'Yes!' A momentary glint of relief lit Ralph's eyes. 'My sister is Serena's guardian and trustee . . .'

'And was married to Serena's father.' Sean's voice was clipped and cold. 'How did you come to lose Serena, by the way?'

Ralph hesitated. 'It was a . . . silly misunderstanding,' he said finally, glancing with affectionate exasperation at Serena and then sending Sean a man-to-man we-know-how-temperamental-these-young-girls-can-be look. 'My sister is extremely fond of Serena,' he added, 'and only wants what's best for her.'

'Or you?'

Ralph looked innocently enquiring.

'Serena's version is a little different,' Sean said idly.

At once the wary alertness returned to Ralph's expression.

'Serena, in fact,' Sean continued, 'believes that you and your sister planned by one means or another to . . . achieve a marriage between you and her, thereby bringing her considerable inheritance within your grasp.'

Ralph turned his head to Serena, 'You little bitch,' he said softly and menacingly.

Serena shrank back in her chair.

There was dead silence in the study for a moment, then Ralph, sensing that he'd made a tactical blunder, stood up and started to bluster, but Sean cut him off abruptly.

'Sit down, Taylor,' he said in the coldest voice Serena had ever heard, 'and listen to me, because it's important you get this straight. From now on, you and your sister will leave Serena alone—don't even attempt to have anything to do with her, unless you wish to deal with me.'

'But . . . my sister has rights . . .'

'So does Serena,' Sean cut in. 'And I intend to protect her rights even if it means taking things to court. I don't suppose it would make very pretty hearing—the way you forced your attentions on her until she could see no other course but to run away. Penniless, what's more. In fact there's nothing to stop me instigating proceedings against you now.'

Ralph stood up again, his face a red, sweaty mask of fury. 'Just try it,' he taunted.

'Don't tempt me,' Sean said softly. 'Furthermore, if you ever lay a finger on her again, it will give me great pleasure to give you the thrashing you deserve.'

'You . . . you wouldn't . . .'

'Oh, I would,' said Sean, his grey-green eyes glinting. 'But for now, I'll content myself with throwing you off the property. Bill!' he called, raising his voice and striding to the door.

Bill must have been hovering outside, because the door opened immediately. 'Yes, boss?'

'I want you to fly *Mr* Taylor,' Sean said with a world of contempt, 'to Dalby. He can make his own way from there. Just one thing,' he turned back to Ralph, 'how did you find out Serena was here?'

Several expressions chased across Ralph's face—impotent fury being uppermost. And for a moment it looked as if he wasn't going to oblige. Then Bill moved suggestively into the room, and he said petulantly, 'I don't see what difference it makes, but it was her old headmistress—my sister bumped into her a few days ago and she asked how Serena was getting on in her new job . . .'

'Well, at least that absolves me,' Sean murmured with a wry little glance at Serena, sitting like a statue in her chair. His expression hardened and he turned back to Ralph. 'Out, you . . . lowdown bastard,' he said very quietly, but with so much menace, Ralph went—even hastened.

CHAPTER SIX

SEAN closed the door behind them and came back to Serena. He put his hand on her shoulder. 'It's over now,' he said gently.

But it seemed it wasn't over for Serena. She stood up, wanting to thank him, but no words would come—only tears that soon became racking sobs, and finally, as if it was the most natural thing in the world, when he put his arms around her, she clung to him as if he was the only spar she had in the sea of life.

Eventually he picked her up and sat down in an armchair with her. 'Serena, stop now,' he said at last. 'You'll make yourself sick.' But he continued to stroke her hair.

'I . . . I'm trying,' she hiccupped. 'Thank you for believing me and doing what you did. I'm *so* grateful . . . I just can't think how to repay you!'

Sean grimaced faintly over her head. 'There's no need. It's only what most people would have done.'

'No, it's not. And anyway,' she sniffed, and laid her head on his shoulder, 'I wouldn't feel nearly as safe with anyone else.'

'As to that,' he said slowly, smoothing damp strands of hair that were clinging to her cheek behind her ear, 'I doubt whether Ralph Taylor will bother you again, but we could take him to court if you really wanted to. There's one disadvantage . . .'

'I don't ever want to have to see him again,' she whispered with a shudder.

'That's what I mean. You'd not only have to see him, them, but you'd have to relive it all in graphic detail.'

'If you really don't mind me staying here until I'm twenty-one . . .'

'I've told you I don't. There is another problem, however. I think some sort of check ought to be made just in case your stepmother has other plans for milking the estate somehow. Now you're no longer a minor you could ask for an audit. Would you like me to set that up?'

'Oh, yes! Please.'

'And this sheep station—what's the position there?'

'There's a manager looking after it. He's been there for years and I know my father trusted him. He runs it as if it were his own, sort of.'

'All right. Feeling better now?'

'Mmm . . .'

Sean regarded her unconscious face with its lowered lashes, the way she was touching and idly twisting a button of his shirt, then he looked up to stare across the room unseeingly, his lips twisting at some hidden irony. All he said, though, was, 'I don't know about you, but I'm hungry.'

Serena sat up and clapped a hand to her mouth. 'I put a casserole in the oven—it only needed an hour . . .'

'It's only been an hour.'

'Is that all? I feel as if my whole life has passed in a sort of microcosm. Oh—poor Bill! I feel very guilty about putting him to so much trouble . . . but I'll keep some dinner for him. I never got a chance to ask you, but did you fix that bore?'

'Yes.'

'Good.' Serena slid off his lap and turned to smile down at him. 'I still don't know how to thank you, but I'll really try to be a model governess from now on, so you won't regret what you've done for me.'

'I wouldn't try too hard,' he said gravely but with his eyes amused.

'Why not?'

He shrugged. 'I'd rather you were relaxed about it. Just go on as you have been.'

Serena considered. 'It will certainly be a bit easier now I know you aren't expecting me to . . . to . . . well, wondering if I'm going to pop off with the next man who looks at me.'

'I do apologise for that, but you must admit that without my being a mind-reader, it was a . . . an assumption that seemed worthy.'

Serena considered again.

'At the time,' Sean murmured.

She grimaced. 'I guess so. It's funny really, though.'

He raised an eyebrow.

'Well, I'm just the opposite, actually!'

'That . . . could change.'

'It doesn't feel like it,' she said with a shrug.

'Didn't you ever mix with any boys?' he asked, his eyes oddly watchful and curious.

'Not really—it was an all girls' school I went to, and then . . .'

'When the time came to be interested in boys, Ralph and your stepmother intervened. If you could try to forget about all that, you might find . . . things start to take their natural course.'

Serena thought for a bit. 'You mean my development's been a bit arrested, sort of? Not turned right off? That . . .' She broke off and grinned suddenly.

'What now?'

'I just thought . . . well, that's really funny, you know!'

'No,' Sean said patiently. 'What is?'

'It's almost as if you're saying—you wouldn't mind if I had a boyfriend now, whereas before . . .'

A wry smile tugged at his lips. 'I do see the irony.'

'But I don't think it's going to be a problem,' Serena said blithely. 'Unless I could find someone like . . .' She broke off, her violet eyes widening and a hot tide of colour creeping into her cheeks.

'Find someone . . .?'

'Nothing,' she mumbled. 'I didn't mean . . . oh!' She put her hands to her face in agitation.

'Serena,' he said thoughtfully, his eyes grey and cool, 'what you see in me at the moment,' her eyes flew to his, 'is some sort of father figure—protector.' He waited.

'Yes,' she whispered, 'yes. That must be it.'

Sean smiled faintly. 'And once you get over your excess of gratitude, we'll be back to square one, no doubt. I mean, there'll be times when I make you very cross and vice versa. Like this afternoon.'

'You did . . . did you hear me?' she stammered.

'It wasn't necessary—you were brandishing your fist at me.'

'I *wasn't!* Was I?' she asked guiltily.

'It was a very similar gesture,' he replied, his eyes alight with laughter.

Serena stared at him, filled with a mixture of emotions, then despite herself, she had to laugh.

Sean stood up and ruffled her hair. 'That's better—we'll just go on as before, shall we? And in the meantime, your casserole could be getting overcooked now.'

Serena started. 'I keep forgetting the wretched thing! I'll go . . . just one thing,' she added determinedly, not moving an inch, 'whatever, I'll *always* be in your debt, and nothing you can say will make me change my mind!'

'Then I won't even try,' he assured her.

She cast him a doubtful look, feeling baffled and as if there must be *some* way she could make him take her seriously, but as he folded his arms across his chest and raised an eyebrow at her, discretion seemed to be wiser than valour, and she left the study with dignity.

But despite Sean's efforts to restore things to normal, some curious reactions set to work in Serena's mind almost immediately. One was nothing new—that same feeling of being on the brink of something she couldn't fathom gripped her again, although now she did know it concerned Sean. The other reaction definitely concerned Sean, and it manifested itself the very next morning over breakfast, which for once Sean ate with her.

'This is unusual,' Serena remarked as she dished him up bacon and eggs. 'I got up at the crack to make you something, but only Bill went out.'

'Mmm . . .' was all Sean returned for a time, then he looked across the table at her. 'Serena, I was supposed to go to Brisbane yesterday—Coast, actually—on business, but I postponed it . . .'

'I know . . . er . . . Denny told me,' she said quickly.

'Well, I had a phone call late last night and I can't postpone it any longer. I'm flying down this morning.'

'Fly?' She stared at him with her lips parted.

'Bill will be here—I'm flying myself down—and Susie Jones will come up to stay with you at night.'

'Oh.'

'Serena, Ralph is not going to come back,' Sean said deliberately.

'No.'

'Serena . . .'

'It's all right,' she said, getting up. 'I'll be fine.' She piled up some plates and took them through to the kitchen.

He followed her. 'Why are you looking so pale and scared, then?'

'I . . . I didn't know I was. Bill,' she paused, 'Bill will be out and about a lot. Can I go with him?'

'Yes, if you want to. You do know you'd be as safe with Bill as me?'

'Of course—there's nothing to worry about! I was just being foolish.'

'Yes,' Sean said quietly.

Serena sat on the floor in her bedroom, playing with Rupert and listening for the plane to take off. When what she did hear finally was a Land Rover stopping at the garden gate, she assumed it was Bill.

But they didn't sound like Bill's footsteps, those that she heard through the house, coming towards her bedroom, and she frowned and glanced up at the same time as Sean appeared in the doorway.

She gasped. 'You! But . . . has something gone wrong?'

Sean regarded her expressionlessly for about ten seconds, then he said, 'You've got five minutes to throw some things into a suitcase.'

'A . . . but I don't understand!'

'It's quite simple,' he said with dry patience, 'I'm taking you with me.'

'But . . . *why?*'

'If you must know, the thought of you sitting here all lost and forlorn activated my . . . er . . . conscience. Are you going to pack, or must I do it for you?'

'Sean . . .' Serena got up. 'I can't come . . .'

Sean cast his eyes heavenwards and ground his teeth visibly. 'Why not?'

'I feel . . . *my* conscience has been activated and,' she stopped a little helplessly and bent down to pick up Rupert as he curled himself around her ankle, 'and anyway, there's Rupert,' she added.

'You mean this undersized cat?'

'Actually he's doubled his size, but I still have to feed him frequently.'

'Bring him,' Sean said laconically.

'Sean . . .'

'Serena,' Sean eyed her dangerously, 'just bring him . . . in a basket or something, I'm running late as it is.'

'But I feel awful now,' she cried.

'You surprise me—I thought you were scared stiff of being left here without me?'

Serena blushed. 'It's just . . . well, it was only yesterday and I was dreaming about Ralph last night, you see, but in time I'll . . . I'm sure I'll . . .'

'Then in the meantime just do as you're told,' commanded Sean. 'That's an order from your employer, incidentally—and his patience is wearing thin.'

'Well . . .'

Sean swore softly.

'I'm coming!'

'I've just thought of something,' Serena said worriedly after take-off.

Sean raised an eyebrow.

'They may object to a cat—even one as undersized as this one—at a hotel.'

'We're not staying at a hotel.'

'We're not?'

'No. A cousin of mine and his wife have a house on the Isle of Capri at the Gold Coast. We'll be staying there.'

'Will they mind—about me?'

'I shouldn't think so. They have no children, Des and Lorraine, and consequently they love other people's.'

'I'm not . . .'

'You're still young enough to qualify on one count—Lorraine is just old enough to be your mother.'

'Oh.'

'So while Des and I conduct business, you and Lorraine can windowshop . . . whatever you like.'

'I see,' Serena said slowly.

'You don't approve?'

'Yes!'

'Good,' Sean said briskly. 'Any more concerns?'

'I . . . no,' she said.

'I'd rather you were honest with me,' he remarked,

a dry little smile twisting his lips.

Serena bit her lip. 'It's just . . . well, I feel a terrible nuisance and I know you're irritated with me—not that I blame you in the slightest,' she hastened to assure him. 'But I'd just rather be in your good books,' she added barely audibly.

Sean was silent, concentrating on his flying, and after a while, Serena looked out of her window unseeingly, wishing she hadn't said it and feeling guilty and foolish.

Then he took one hand off the controls and covered her tightly clenched hands with it. 'Relax, little one,' he said soothingly. 'You are in my good books. I just have a naturally abrasive personality sometimes.'

The burst of sheer happiness that flooded Serena manifested itself in a radiant smile.

He smiled back rather wryly.

'Rupert,' Serena said, as she got ready for dinner that night, 'I feel like pinching myself. Here I am—we are—in the lap of luxury and being treated just like family, what's more.'

She looked around the guest bedroom in Des and Lorraine Wentworth's Isle of Capri home. It was all white and lacy except for the sulphur yellow carpet and decorated especially for female guests, whereas the bedroom Sean had, which she had glimpsed through the open door, was decidedly, although luxuriously, masculine.

Whether or not Sean had explained the circumstances of her presence, she wasn't sure, but his cousin Des and Lorraine had apparently been delighted to have her, and had assured her that they wouldn't dream of her not attending the small party they were holding that evening.

'Therein lies a problem, though, Rupert,' Serena explained to the little cat, contentedly curled up in his basket, as she scanned the contents of her suitcase which she had upended on to the bed. 'I had to pack in such a hurry I didn't even think of including something even remotely elegant enough to wear to a party here.'

She sat down on the bed and worriedly bit the tip of her forefinger. For everything about this beautiful house shouted restrained elegance to her—not only that, her hostess was the epitome of it.

She jumped at the sound of a light tap on her door and nervously called 'come in'.

It was Lorraine, blonde and svelte but with unusually kind blue eyes—perhaps I could just be truthful with her, Serena thought as she returned Lorraine's smile.

'I . . . would you mind very much if I didn't come to your party?' she said breathlessly. 'It's . . . just that I don't have a thing to wear! We left in such a hurry and I didn't even know where I was going . . . sort of.'

'My dear,' Lorraine closed the door behind her, 'yes, I would mind! And I'm sure I could find something for you to wear.'

'Oh, but . . .'

'In fact that's why I'm here. It occurred to Sean that you wouldn't have packed a lot. Now, let's see,' she studied Serena intently, 'I'm a little taller and bit . . . broader,' her eyes twinkled humorously, 'but one can achieve marvels with *belts* these days, you know . . . you can take up the slack and blouse it out, sort of thing. What say I go and get a couple of outfits and we'll see what we can do?'

'Well,' Serena said uncertainly, but Lorraine was gone.

'There,' murmured Lorraine, some time later, 'how about that?'

The image in the mirror that gazed back at Serena was young, grave and very elegant in a beautiful two-piece outfit of an ivory overblouse with padded shoulders and long, tight sleeves worn belted and bloused over a billowing amethyst skirt. Her hair was tied back in the nape of her neck with a matching amethyst bow.

Serena blinked.

'Don't you like it?' Lorraine enquired.

'I love it,' Serena replied in a slightly awed voice. 'It makes me feel . . . I don't know—yes, I do! It makes me feel like Delvene.'

Lorraine laughed. 'Is that an ambition of yours?'

'I just thought she was so . . . well, whatever she wore, she looked good enough to be in *Vogue* . . .'

'Then I have to agree—you do look as if you could have stepped out of the pages of *Vogue*.'

Serena turned away from the mirror. 'You're so kind,' she said huskily. 'I don't know how to thank you—I mean, you barely know me, and I am only the governess!'

Lorraine patted her cheek. 'Sean said you were more than a governess, he said you were part of the family.'

'Sean,' Serena's voice trembled slightly, 'is . . . I'll be in his debt for ever.'

Lorraine looked slightly taken aback and she said thoughtfully after a moment, 'I have to confess you've aroused my curiosity, Serena.'

'He . . . he saved me from a terrible fate,' Serena told her with a shudder. 'Two, in fact.'

'Two terrible fates?' Lorraine asked quizzically.

'I know it sounds . . . strange, but it's true. I thought he might have told you? And that's why you're being so kind?'

'He hasn't—well, only that Richard and Cameron and Mrs Denby have gone to Sydney with Delvene, so you're at a loose end—but if I was curious before I'm positively agog now!'

Perhaps because she'd bottled it all up inside her for so long, Serena found herself telling Lorraine everything, although briefly.

'But how *awful* for you!' Lorraine exclaimed, her expression genuinely horrified and concerned. 'My dear child . . . I'm speechless!'

'Perhaps you can understand how I feel about Sean now,' Serena said seriously and confidingly. 'I'd do anything for him.'

Lorraine's eyes narrowed briefly as she absorbed the unconscious fervour of Serena's expression. 'I . . . yes, of course I understand,' she said slowly. 'Tell me, what did you think of Delvene? Apart from her ability to wear clothes, that is?'

Serena blinked at this apparent change of subject. 'Oh . . . I liked her! I mean, she can't help being the way she is, but I'm sure she cares for the twins and I think it's just a pity she and Sean—well, can't bury their differences, seeing that they *both* care for them so much.'

It was Lorraine's turn to blink and hesitate until she said, 'Yes . . .'

'Don't you like Delvene?' Serena enquired.

Lorraine hesitated again, then sighed. 'It's hard. We were all so fond of Andrew, you see.'

'Yes,' Serena agreed understandingly. 'I know I've thought before that if he'd been my brother, I might not have been able to see things so impartially. Well,' she swung back to the mirror so that her skirt twirled out gracefully, 'I'm ready! Is there anything I can do to help? Please let me—I'd feel less guilty about gatecrashing your party, let alone your wardrobe, if you did!'

'I . . . I was just going to put the finishing touches to some savouries and then have a lightning change myself . . .'

'I can do that,' Serena said firmly. 'All I need is an apron.'

Sean was the first person Serena encountered after she had achieved what she thought of as such a metamorphosis in Lorraine's clothes.

She had just put the finishing touches to the savouries as artistically as she was able, she had rinsed her hands and taken off her apron and was standing admiring her handiwork in the blue and white kitchen, when Sean strolled in wearing a navy blue suit, white shirt and with a paler blue and grey striped tie in his hands.

'Oh!' Serena exclaimed, her violet eyes running over him. 'You look different!'

'Better or worse?' he asked with a flicker of amusement.

Serena considered, taking in his well brushed tawny hair and well polished black leather shoes, her eyes lingering on the crisp white handkerchief in his jacket pocket. Then she smiled. 'Not better or worse, but it's as if you're two people . . . the down here you and the up there you. Sort of . . . someone I don't know very well, not nearly as well as I know the up there at Rosewood you, but very handsome!'

'Permit me to return the compliment. You appear to be a new you too.'

He walked round her, then leant back against a counter and pulled his tie through his fingers.

'Don't you like it?'

'I do.'

Serena grinned. 'I'd rather you were honest with me,' she murmured, and looked at him through her lashes.

He smiled faintly. 'All right. You look lovely: rather sophisticated, but at the same time . . . as if you're about attend the Sunday school picnic—a perhaps dangerous combination.'

For a moment Serena looked, if anything, mortally offended, then she started to giggle. 'If I do,' she said at last, 'look as if I'm going to the Sunday school picnic—which I take to mean looking full of joyful, childish anticipation—it's only because I feel as if I've had the weight of the world lifted off my shoulders and because everyone is being so unbelievably nice to me! But I don't see what can be dangerous about that.'

'That's the problem,' he said drily, but as Serena's face fell, he straightened and came over to her to touch her cheek lightly. 'Enjoy yourself, petal. You certainly deserve to.'

*   *   *

An hour later, Des and Lorraine's beautiful lounge, which was decorated in lime green and a variety of hibiscus pinks, was thronged with people. Serena had been introduced to many of them . . . simply as Serena St John, with no mention being made of the fact that she was an employee of Sean's. She'd thought to add this information herself, but had thought then that it might sound curiously gauche.

Nor had she been aware of the reason for holding this party until Des had tapped on his glass for silence, and made a small speech.

'Friends,' he'd said, 'thank you all for coming, especially as it was such short notice. In fact it was Lorraine's idea to celebrate a . . . well, quite a milestone for us. Which is, that milestone, that Sean and I in partnership, have today purchased Witawonga Downs station . . .'

There was a collective gasp around the room, then Des and Sean were besieged by a flurry of congratulations.

'As you all know—and I'm sorry if I sound smug,' Des said ruefully when the tumult had subsided, 'this is quite a feather in our cap, not only because of the history attached to Witawonga but because it will increase our pastoral holdings substantially. I must add,' he went on, overriding the hear-hears, 'that my cousin Sean should take most of the credit for this being possible. Because it's been his excellent steward-ship of Rosewood and consequently our increased profits that have put us in the position of being able to buy Witawonga. I give you Sean Wentworth!'

Through the hearty cheers that followed, Serena gazed at Sean wide-eyed, and felt as if her heart might burst with pride. He was smiling faintly, that rather wry smile she knew so well, but he also looked relieved when Lorraine came to his rescue with the announcement that a light supper was being served. And once again, she was conscious of that *being on the brink of some great discovery* feeling, which caused her to frown in frustration.

That it should hit her—the explanation for this feeling—right out of the blue during supper, took her so much by surprise at first, she felt dizzy. A moment or two later, she couldn't understand how she could have been so blind, though.

She was watching Sean again, but this time he was talking to a gorgeous woman in her early thirties, Serena guessed, a vivid brunette wearing dull gold and with intelligence, sophistication and class written all over her. But what really arrested Serena was something in Sean's heavy-lidded gaze as it rested on the woman, who was talking animatedly. He . . . he's interested in her, she thought. He's . . . attracted and finds her desirable . . . oh God! Why does that make me feel . . . just miserable?

The answer was not long in coming and she turned away, her mind reeling with the knowledge that she had done the impossible—on two counts. She had fallen in love when she had foolishly thought it couldn't happen to her, but she had also fallen head over heels in love with Sean Wentworth.

Oh, how I deluded myself! she marvelled bitterly. Even . . . even after Ralph, when I said what I did, I persuaded myself that he must he right, that he'd become a father figure . . . did he guess?

She closed her eyes in horror and turned away jerkily—to bump into a tall dark man standing right behind her.

'Sorry,' she whispered.

'No problem,' the man answered. 'In fact I've been wanting to talk to you, because I'm sure we've met somewhere.'

Serena glanced at him distractedly. 'I don't think so.'

'Then let me introduce myself—Reg Findlay. I used to go to school with Sean. Hey,' he said softly, 'you look a little pale. It's a bit hot in here now—what say I get you a fresh drink and we take it out on to the veranda?'

'I . . . well, thank you. Just something soft.'

The air on the terrace, which overlooked the Nerang River, was fresh and cool, and moonlight glinted on the water as a mullet jumped and spread a circle of widening ripples.

'Better?' Reg Findlay enquired.

'Yes—thank you very much.' Serena sipped her lemonade, but there was still a dazed uncomprehending look in her eyes.

'You're a friend of Sean's?' Reg Findlay asked casually.

'I work for him.'

'Do you now—in what capacity?'

Something in his voice caused a wriggle of unease in Serena, but when she turned to look at him his expression was only bland and politely enquiring.

'I'm . . . the governess. For Richard and Cameron.'

'Ah! Delvene's kids . . . so you live up at Rosewood? With Sean?'

'Yes. Yes, I do,' Serena agreed, but uncertainly, because he was now smiling broadly down at her—a curiously unpleasant smile. 'W-what is it?' she stammered.

'Just that I wouldn't have believed it of Sean,' drawled Reg Findlay. 'He's always assumed a rather high moral character—even Delvene ran headlong into it.' He shrugged. 'Still,' he gazed down at Serena in a way that brought the blood to her cheeks, 'you're lovely enough to tempt the best of us—I thought that when I first laid eyes on you a couple of months ago.'

An awful suspicion came to Serena, causing her to go as pale as she'd been red, suddenly. 'What do you mean?' she whispered.

'I'm talking about the Pelican Club, sweetheart. You did work there once, didn't you? I've never forgotten those violet eyes.'

'Please!'

But Reg Findlay was not to be stopped, and Serena realised too late that he was between her and the door, so her only avenue of escape was to climb over the terrace railing . . . She shrank away from him against a wall as he continued,

'I guess if Sean wants to use the term *governess* to . . . cover your services, that's really rather ingenious, because I'm damn sure he'd no more hire a governess, a real governess, out of a place like that than he'd fly. I don't suppose he'd take the governess to a party like this either . . . You must,' he paused thoughtfully, 'be pretty crash hot in bed, honey, for him to go these lengths, especially when he's had the pick of the crop for years—but listen,' he put his hands on Serena's shoulders and pulled her towards him so that his breath fanned her face, 'if you ever get tired of him, give me a ring—I'm in the book—because you'd find me an exciting and generous lover, honey, and what's more I wouldn't expect you to masquerade as a governess . . .'

Serena closed her eyes, but they flew open an instant later at a sound—and before her horrified gaze Sean loomed up behind Reg Findlay, almost lazily grasped Findlay's shoulder and turned him away from her—then formed his free hand into a fist and crashed it into Reg Rindlay's mouth.

She made an inarticulate little sound as Findlay slumped backwards, knocking over a wrought-iron table and ending up flat on his back. Her eyes flew to Sean, then jerked to the lighted doorway that led to the lounge to see a flock of horrified, incredulous guests peering out . . . She thought, as their gazes switched to her and registered varying degrees of speculation, that she could die right there on the spot . . . and with a convulsive movement she took refuge in flight, stumbling towards the door, evading Sean's grasp, and the crowd of people at the door parted to let her through.

She ran across the lounge and upstairs to the yellow and white bedroom, closing the door and leaning against it panting for breath for a moment. Then she pushed herself away from it and grabbed her suitcase and put it, open, on the bed.

Lorraine didn't bother to knock, and by the time she arrived, Serena's suitcase was packed, except for a pair of jeans and a sweater that lay on the bed, and she'd taken off the beautiful ivory and amethyst outfit and was standing in the middle of the room in her silk and lace camisole top and half petticoat.

'My dear child!' Lorraine exclaimed, crossing the carpet towards her.

Serena turned a white, agonised face to her. 'I . . . I'm going,' she whispered. 'Please don't try to stop me.'

'But *why?* You . . .'

'You don't understand,' Serena interrupted. 'I . . . I've disgraced Sean, and it will always be the same. Not only that, I'm nothing but *trouble* . . .'

The door opened again and Sean came in, surveyed the scene for a moment, the way Serena turned away jerkily, and said, 'Thanks, Lorraine—I'll handle this.'

Lorraine hesitated briefly, then she walked out.

'Serena,' Sean said very quietly, 'listen to me.'

'I . . . I can't . . .'

'Yes, you can. You see, I've changed my mind,' he said, and waited.

'Changed your mind . . .?' Serena groped for understanding, still with her back turned to him. 'What about?'

'About us getting married. So you'd better unpack.'

CHAPTER SEVEN

SERENA went rigid.

'Getting married?' she whispered.

'Mmm . . . I think it's a good idea, for several reasons.'

'Sean!' She turned to him at last. 'No . . . please don't,' she implored. 'It's best if I just go.'

He scanned her dazed, horrified expression, the way she was clutching Lorraine's outfit to her, the amethyst bow still in her hair, and his lips twisted. 'Don't you even want to hear my reasons? Besides, it was your idea, originally.'

'That was . . . that was panic talking,' she stammered. 'There can't be *any* reasons for us . . . for us . . '

He strolled towards her, but she backed away and said again in a strangled voice, 'No, please!'

'What do you think I'm going to do?'

'I don't know . . . Sean . . .' But he wrested the clothes from her and observing her sudden despairing glance downwards at her state of undress, he picked up the white towelling robe that came with the room, from the bed and handed it to her.

She scrambled into it, and while she was still doing up the sash, he steered her to the chair in front of the dressing table. 'Sit down,' he ordered.

She sat, and he leant one shoulder against the wall beside the dressing-table and folded his arms as he watched her tragic, totally confused expression.

Then he grimaced. 'The end of the world hasn't come, little one.'

'It feels like it to me,' Serena whispered despairingly.

'Because I want to marry you?'

'But I don't understand!' Her eyes flew to his. '*Why?*'

Sean glanced down at his hand, the hand he had hit Reg Findlay with, and a flicker of amusement lit his grey-green eyes. 'I might not make middle age otherwise,' he commented. 'At least if everyone knows you're mine, they'll back off.'

'Oh, don't joke about it,' Serena begged. 'And everyone will be horrified if you do . . . marry me, I mean. He . . . he won't keep it to himself now . . . did you hear . . .'

'Most of it,' said Sean.

'Well . . . and anyway, there could be *hundreds* of other men out there who . . . it could keep happening!' Serena said with a shudder, then she added, 'Not that it's a possibility anyway.'

'It isn't?' he queried with a lift of an eyebrow.

'No,' she said sadly, 'because I'm going to go away. And nothing you can say will stop me, Sean.' She looked at him with tears but determination in her eyes.

He straightened and said softly, 'Well, if you won't allow me to *state* my reasons, I'll have to show you. You know, you let me kiss you once, petal, when you thought you were considerably turned off men.' He reached down for her hand and drew her to her feet.

'Sean!' she gasped.

'I know,' he said wryly. 'I actually *stole* that

kiss, but for a little while, before you got all cross and hard done by, you were . . . intrigued. Well, I'm going to take it a step further, because I think the passage of time and the fact that you . . . trust me now might prove quite a revelation.'

'Sean . . . Sean,' she whispered, going hot and cold, but he pulled her into his arms with a faint smile, and said, 'Incidentally, I don't at all favour the idea of someone else continuing your instruction in these matters.'

Later, when Serena's breathing had steadied at last, Sean picked her up and carried her across to the bed. He put her down, pushed the suitcase off and pulled the pillows up behind her, then took his shoes and his jacket off and lay down beside her, gathering her into his arms again.

She lay against him, trembling, and troubled at the things she had given away . . . the fact that his touch on her, his gentle, expert kisses, aroused her and made her want to respond . . . In fact she had, incredibly, once he had somehow stilled her fear. To the extent that there could be no doubt in his mind that she, Serena St John, had fallen in love with him because all she had stopped short of was actually saying it.

Perhaps I can explain, she thought tearfully.

'Sean?' she whispered.

'Mmm?' He stroked her hair.

'Sean,' she pulled free and knelt up on the bed, staring down at him, her eyes huge and shadowed to almost purple, 'so . . . so many things have happened in the last couple of days.'

He pushed a hand behind his head and regarded her

quizzically.

'Well,' she licked her lips, 'perhaps . . . because I don't know whether I'm on my head or my heels . . . this has happened.'

'What?'

'You . . . you know what I mean. This!'

'Us, you mean?' he asked lazily.

'Sean,' she said desperately, 'only *yesterday* you told me I was too young for you, not your type, and that I didn't—well . . .'

'Turn me on? Actually, *you* told *me* all that, Serena. And you didn't give me a chance to confirm or deny it,' he returned.

'But you wouldn't even consider marrying me then!'

'I didn't think you'd fallen in love with me then,' he said. 'Not properly.'

'I . . . oh, you did! I think you knew before I did. Didn't you?' Serena asked accusingly, then bit her lip and blushed.

Sean's lips twisted, but his eyes were watchful and acute. 'Doesn't it seem as if we're splitting hairs, Serena?'

'No,' she whispered. 'It means that even if I have . . . fallen in love with you, which is a real miracle, you know . . .'

'I do know.'

'But it *doesn't* mean you've fallen in love with me—that's what I'm trying to say!'

He reached up and released the amethyst bow from which her hair was escaping in tendrils anyway. 'You're wrong there, I do love you,' he said very quietly.

'But . . . but I don't understand,' she stammered.
'I'm sure I'm too young for you—I think,' she said
stubbornly, 'it's best if we forget we ever had this
conversation. What you might love about me is only
what you would feel for a . . . perhaps a sister or
anyone who seems to be having a run of bad luck!'

'I don't go around wanting to make love to everyone
I meet who's having a run of bad luck,' he observed.

Serena trembled. 'Until tonight you've shown no
sign of . . . of that.'

'Nor do I go around making love to little girls who
are frightened out of their wits of men,' he said drily.
'Serena . . .'

'Sean,' she whispered, 'you've been so good to me,
I know you must . . . well, you must have taken a
liking to me, but that's not a good enough reason to
want to marry me. Please, won't you be honest with
me?'

He sat up, pulled off his tie and ran a hand through
his hair. 'All right . . . I think we need each *other* . . .
no, listen to me,' he said gently as Serena trembled
and tried to speak. 'You need a protector—I know, we
could have gone on as before, but it would be rather
ridiculous now, don't you think? And I need . . .' He
stopped and studied her sombrely. 'Serena, something
happened to me once which, while not nearly so
dramatic as your experiences, all the same had a rather
devastating effect on me. It left me . . . cynical and
disenchanted with love.'

Serena's lips parted. 'You . . . you mean you fell in
love with someone you couldn't have or . . . someone
who didn't want you?' she whispered, her eyes
stunned.

'Well,' a mocking glint came to his eye, 'something like that.'

'I *wondered* about that . . .'

'I remember,' he said ironically.

'So . . .? I can't imagine anyone not wanting you, all the same, but . . .'

Sean's lips twitched. 'Thank you,' he said gravely, however. 'And . . .'

But a dawning look of comprehension had come to Serena's violet eyes. 'Now you'd like to marry someone you . . . trust rather than someone you're madly in love with? Is that it?' she queried huskily.

His eyes narrowed and he was silent for a moment. Then he said, 'And like very much and care about.'

'Oh.' It was Serena's turn to be silent as she stared down at the white bedspread. 'This other . . . woman, is there no hope?' she asked.

'None,' he said quietly but so definitely and with an almost . . . what kind of note in his voice? she wondered. Implacable?

She looked up at last and said with a catch in her voice, 'Could . . . could we make it work?'

'I could—if you thought you could,' he replied. Then, seeing the confusion in her eyes, he added, 'What I once thought of as love was actually a kind of madness. This . . . us, as you put it just now, is a very sweet kind of sanity, I think. Don't you think it makes good sense?'

'Sean . . .'

'From your point of view, you even told me once that you thought I had a lot to offer.'

Serena blushed. 'That . . .'

'From my point of view,' he continued, 'apart from

the obvious, there's the fact that we have a lot in common. You love the kind of life I lead, and now there's Witawonga to get to know and make plans for and . . . other plans to make.' He reached out and cupped her cheek. 'I'm sure such a good governess would make a great mother one day.'

'Oh, Sean,' she whispered, and thought of the loneliness of the past couple of years, and the fear. She thought of having her own children to care for, her very own family, she thought of being able to live with Sean and love him, but . . .

'I don't know what to do,' she said at last, her eyes tortured.

'Well, I do,' Sean responded, and pulled her back into his arms. But when she went to bury her face in his shoulder, he tilted her chin up, then slid his fingers caressingly beneath her robe, beneath the strap of her camisole top, and bent his head to kiss her.

CHAPTER EIGHT

SERENA opened her eyes and found herself staring into Sean's.

'Hi,' he said.

'Hi,' she whispered back.

'All right?' he queried.

'I think so.'

He smiled slightly.

'I mean I'm fine,' Serena amended, 'it's just that . . . well, it's something I've never done before, so if I feel a little strange, I'm sure it will pass . . .' She stopped awkwardly. 'Not that I didn't like it! But . . . no, nothing,' she said hastily.

'My dear Serena,' Sean said lazily, 'please tell me what's on your mind or I'll be wondering if you're having second thoughts because I'm a lousy lover.'

'Oh, not you!' she assured him anxiously. 'But I couldn't help remembering something you said to me once, that's all.'

'All? Now I'm really worried,' he murmured, sliding his arms around her slender, naked body. 'Tell me,' he commanded softly.

'Well . . . it was something about my . . . immature, schoolgirlish charms,' she mumbled into his shoulder.

She felt him laugh. 'I only said that to reassure *you*—if you remember, at the time, you thought I'd organised Richard to be at his recalcitrant best, your

147

horse to bolt with you and that I'd commanded a flood all for the express purpose of seducing you.'

Serena winced, then had to giggle. 'All the same,' she said shyly after a moment, 'it was a very . . . demoralising thing to have said to one.'

'In spite of the fact you would have fought me like a young tigress if I'd put one foot or said one word wrong? Of course!' he agreed gravely.

'You know what I mean!' she said reproachfully, although she was still smiling.

'I think I do,' he murmured, moving her away from him. 'You're inviting me to redress that grave injustice I did you . . . very well.' He threw the sheet aside, catching Serena by surprise so that she tensed and made a small, inarticulate sound, but Sean took no notice.

'Where shall I start?' He glanced down the length of her body. 'These?' He touched her small high breasts and Serena shivered as her body was invaded by sensations she'd never known—until last night. 'They're,' Sean continued almost absently, 'exquisite, especially when they . . . ah, do this.'

'Oh,' Serena whispered, feeling her nipples harden and become hot, 'don't!'

'Don't you like it?' he queried softly.

'Yes,' she gasped, 'no—I don't know. It's very hard to explain, but it seems to make my whole body feel very . . . sensitive. What are you doing now?' she asked, catching and arresting his hand as it moved down to her waist.

Sean stared down at her, his grey-green eyes curiously enigmatic, then they softened. 'I was going to carry on cataloguing your charms so you wouldn't feel schoolgirlish and immature, but I think we'll take it more slowly. I'll tell you instead,' he said with a flicker of a smile. 'You're beautiful, Serena, and very desirable—I doubt if anyone would dispute that.'

Her eyes were shy again as she returned his gaze. 'I'm also . . . very inexperienced—I guess that was obvious?'

'Virgins usually are,' he commented, and slid his hand through her hair. 'It's part of their charm. Don't worry so much,' he added with a faint grin. 'Tell you what, let's have a bet that in—say, a couple of weeks—you won't be worrying about your inexperience. And in the meantime, we have a decision to make.'

'We do?'

'Mmm.' He kissed her lightly on the lips. 'This is the first day of our married life, not to mention our honeymoon, so we have to plan how to spend it. We could either stay here all day . . .'

'In bed!'

'I'm sure it's been done,' he replied with a wicked glint in his eye. 'Or we could get up . . . for a while.'

'Sean,' Serena said softly, lifting her arms and sliding them around his neck, 'one thing I have learnt through associating with you is that you often tease me wickedly!'

He raised an eyebrow and said with the utmost gravity, 'Want to bet?'

Nearly a fortnight later, Serena was sitting cross-legged on Des and Lorraine's bed with a bowl of grapes in her lap. Like the rest of the Isle of Capri house, the master bedroom, done in lilac and silver, was a decorator's dream, with the ultimate luxury being the the four-poster canopied bed upon which Serena was sitting, clad only in her robe and eating her grapes as late afternoon sunlight flooded the bedroom.

And once again the luxury of this bedroom brought to mind the generosity of its owners.

'You know,' she said to Sean as he came out of the en suite bathroom with only a towel draped around his hips, 'I still can't get over how *kind* everyone is, especially Des and Lorraine. I mean, organising that lovely little wedding at such short notice, lending us their house for our honeymoon and going up to Rosewood to look after Richard and Cameron. They even managed to look happy about you marrying me.'

Sean grinned. 'Lorraine's been trying to marry me off for years.'

'Not to a perfect stranger, someone who also caused a *fight* at her party and . . .'

'She must have liked you in spite of it all,' Sean said humorously.

Serena considered, popping a succulent green grape into her mouth. 'Still,' she said finally, 'it must have surprised a lot of people. Delvene, for instance. I wonder what she thinks about it?'

'I doubt if she even knows,' Sean said carelessly, coming to sit on the end of the bed.

'Oh?'

'She was due to go off on tour before it actually happened.'

'Oh. Sean,' Serena wrinkled her brow and ate another grape, 'I'm worried about something.'

'I've never known anyone to find so much to worry about—or to have such a consuming passion for grapes,' he remarked wryly. 'What is it this time?'

Serena sighed. 'It's Denny—what *will* she think of me! And Bill—they must have been so surprised.'

'It's possible they might think worse of me.'

'You?' Serena stared at him.

'Petal, some people could accuse me of cradle-snatching.'

Serena pursed her lips and said primly, 'I'll be nineteen in a month. And I was also worried about that,' she reminded him. 'Only from *your* point of view, if you know what I mean.'

'Oh, I do,' he drawled, and removed the bowl of grapes from her lap. 'You'll spoil your dinner if you eat too many more of those—besides, I want to show you something.'

'What?' Serena enquired innocently as he drew back the cover and motioned her to slip beneath it.

He slid in beside her. 'Just how mature, even inspired you've become lately,' he said softly as he released the sash of her robe and opened it.

'I've just had my shower, Sean,' she said demurely as he ran his hands over her body.

'Even matronly,' he teased. 'There's no charge for hot water here.'

'We're going out for dinner shortly,' she reminded him. 'We have reservations.'

'Positively *wifely*,' he commented. 'Certainly much less shy and worried—about this at least. Did we or did we not have a bet at the start of this honeymoon?'

'Well,' Serena said cautiously, as he eased his weight on to her, 'before I concede that, you didn't mention what was involved for the winner and the . . . loser.'

'Oh, there's a dreadful penalty involved for the . . . loser.' His eyes glinted.

'I thought there might be.' She pretended to consider. 'A kiss behind the shed?'

'Worse.'

'A kiss and a cuddle? *Much* against my will, of course, but a bet is a bet.' She freed a hand and fiddled with the tawny hair falling over Sean's brow. 'You know, I used to wonder about being . . . like this. I thought it would be really uncomfortable, having a man lying on top of you. It didn't seem . . . practical, because men are generally *heavier*. But it's rather nice, in fact.'

His eyes narrowed. 'Only rather? And are you trying to evade the issue, by any chance? If so I must tell you you're going about it the wrong way. A kiss and a cuddle won't nearly satisfy me now.'

'I never thought they would,' Serena said pertly. 'I knew right from the start that you were going to have your way with me . . . men who make bets like that generally do.'

'Have their way?'

'Uh-huh.' Her lips trembled.

'In your experience?'

'Oh, yes.'

'Do you know something?' he queried. 'You're growing up *so* fast, you've even surprised me.'

'I think my teacher should take the credit . . . or the blame for that,' she said seriously. 'What do you think?'

'I think I might have to think up a penalty for sheer impudence.'

Serena's lips trembled again, but this time she

couldn't control her laughter.

'Right this minute,' he murmured.

'Oh, I'm ready and waiting.'

In the end they had to change their dinner reservations for a later hour, and have another shower.

After dinner, Sean stopped the Mercedes along the beachfront on the way home. It was a bright, clear night with a definite chill in the air, but not nearly as cold as it would be at Rosewood now. The surf was curling into the beach below almost lazily and the moon hung in the sky, silvering the ocean.

Serena put her head on Sean's shoulder. 'It's so beautiful,' she murmured.

'Yes . . . Home tomorrow, but I thought we might make a short detour on the way.'

'Where to?'

'Witawonga—would you like to see it?'

'I'd love to.'

'Good . . . you know, you don't have to worry about what Bill and Denny will think, by the way. They're both rather wise people, I've found. And not given to passing rash judgements, especially on people they like.'

Serena half smiled.

'And I can only imagine Richard and Cameron will be thrilled. I had a thought about them, incidentally.'

'Oh?'

'Yes—they'll need another governess now,' he said with a grin.

Serena sat up. 'Sean, I don't mind looking after them! Truly I don't.'

'But they're a full-time job, whereas you could have your hands full.'

'Doing what?'

He raised an eyebrow. 'Being a wife.'

'Lots of wives cope with children too. I'm sure I can, and anyway, they're rather prickly on the subject of governesses. Let's wait and see . . . please?'

'When you say it like that—all right, we'll have a trial period. But if I start to feel neglected . . .'

'I promise you that won't happen!'

'I'll hold you to that,' murmured Sean, and put his arms round her. 'The last time we did this it was raining.'

'No, it wasn't . . . oh, you mean . . .?'

'Yes, and you were covered in grit and wearing a rather revealing outfit.' He let his gaze roam over her, taking in the midnight blue dress she was wearing— amongst other things on their honeymoon, he had bought her nearly a whole new wardrobe—her hair which she had knotted on top of her head in a bid to look more sophisticated, her downcast lashes casting shadows on her cheeks. 'All the same, you were still astonishingly beautiful,' he said quietly.

Her lashes lifted. 'You told me you preferred your women a little older and a lot cleaner,' she whispered.

'I said a lot of thinigs to you once I'm going to have to live down, I can see,' Sean said wryly. 'But there was one thing you used to say to me . . . *frequently*. In the light of it, do you have any regrets now?' He touched her mouth, then slid his fingers down her throat.

Serena laid her head back against his arm so she could stare up at him, into those eyes that had made her shiver with fear once . . . everything about him that had made her feel quite out of his league, a foolish little girl . . . until he had taken her to his bed and released a sensuality she had not known she was capable of, to add to her love. I'll love him till the day I die, she thought. I'll make up for that other woman and one day he'll love me the same way . . .

'No . . . none,' she said huskily, and kissed his fingers as they roamed up to her lips again. 'Do you?'

'No.' He lowered his head and claimed her mouth.

Richard and Cameron's first reaction to Sean and Serena's arrival home was one of astonishment at how Rupert had grown.

'Boy, oh boy!' Cameron said round-eyed. 'Do babies grow that fast?'

'No!' Serena said laughingly. 'What made you think that?'

'Cameron's got them on the mind since you and Sean got married,' Richard said offhandedly. 'Sammy Banks reckons that'll be the the the next step.'

'He does, does he?' drawled Sean as Serena blushed and Des and Lorraine, who were going to spend a few more days at Rosewood, exchanged humorous glances.

'Sammy Banks is a force to be reckoned with!' Des said wryly. 'If you ask me, Serena, you deserve a medal for coping with the trio of them.'

'You probably only know half of it,' Sean returned as they all piled into the Land Rover Des had driven down to the airstrip to meet them.

'How did you cope?' Lorraine asked ruefully, out of the corner of her mouth.

'I mentioned Sean frequently,' Serena replied in a

laughing undertone. 'It always did the trick. How . . . how did they take the news?'

'Very well, actually, although even Richard was surprised. But he did say—at least she'll stay with us now.'

Serena grimaced. 'I . . . and Denny?'

'What are you two girls whispering about?' Des asked.

'Nothing . . . girl talk, that's all,' Lorraine answered airily, but the opportunity was lost to find out how Denny had reacted to the news because they had arrived at the homestead. And Serena's heart sank as she noticed Denny and Bill standing at the garden gate like a reception committee.

Sean reached for her hand and squeezed it reassuringly.

But if Mrs Denby had any reservations about this out-of-the-blue marriage, she chose not to show them. Instead, she folded Serena into her arms and hugged her warmly, then turned to Sean with tears in her eyes and shook his hand. But Sean was not content with that.

'Denny,' he said gravely, 'you've known me for almost as long as I can remember, you've chastised me and called the wrath of God down on my head a few times . . . I think I deserve more than a handshake now!'

Mrs Denby smiled through her tears and stood on tiptoe to kiss him. 'You're right. I hope you'll . . . both be very happy!'

And Bill said to Serena, 'That's a wise choice you made, young 'un!'

*   *   *

Over the next few days, life at the old Rosewood homestead was spirited and happy. And as a relocation period—from governess to mistress of the house—things couldn't have gone more smoothly for Serena. It struck her once that everyone was really going out of their way to ensure this—and struck her that it was extraordinarily kind, if just a little surprising. Everyone's really bending over backwards, she mused. As if they're very determined, *really* determined to make this marriage work. Well, that's understandable now it's done, and considering I'm not far short of a perfect stranger . . . Why does that phrase keep cropping up in mind? But, she pondered, more importantly, is it my imagination, or *is* everyone ultra-anxious to make things easy for me?

She shook her head, and as a natural progression perhaps, her thoughts turned to Sean. He was very relaxed, she thought. Relaxed and . . . tender, even in public, and that had to mean something, hadn't it? Even if she wasn't the love of his life.

'She must have been . . . who could she have been?' she asked aloud with a frown wrinkling her brow. 'And why do I feel like Pandora whenever I think about it?'

'Does she know?'

Serena paused on her way to the main bedroom as she heard Lorraine ask the question of Mrs Denby. They were sitting around the corner of the house on the back steps in a patch of afternoon sunlight, and Serena had realised over the last couple of days that they were friends from way back, Denny and Lorraine, in fact Des and Lorraine had been married from

Rosewood homestead.

'I don't know,' she heard Mrs Denby answer.

'She has to know soon,' said Lorraine. 'What I can't help wondering is what she would do—how she would react.'

'God help me—neither can I!' Mrs Denby agreed.

Are they talking about me? Serena wondered as she found herself unwittingly eavesdropping again. This time she had taken Richard and Cameron down to the creek to fish, but Des and Sean had caught up with her and offered to take her place. Since fishing wasn't something she was much of an expert at, she had laughingly relinquished her post, and declined to stay and be taught. She had ridden Sally home—a fact of which Lorraine and Mrs Denby were obviously unaware as they freely continued their conversation.

'You could have knocked me down with a feather when Sean broke the news that he was going to marry her,' Lorraine said ruefully.

'Me too, when I heard, although . . .'

'I know,' Lorraine cut in, 'she obviously adores him.'

Serena bit her lip.

'He could have done a lot worse,' Mrs Denby said slowly. 'Actually, I think it's the best thing that could have happened to him.'

'I'm tempted to think the same. Innocence, purity, a girl in real distress, from what she told me, and Sean confirmed it. She also apparently has a fortune of her own, so we don't have to worry on that score!'

'There've been plenty of those over the years,' Mrs Denby said drily.

'And there's the fact that Richard and Cameron

dote on her, although Richard would be the last to admit it, but did you see their faces light up when they saw her again? By the way, how *did* they enjoy their stay with Delvene? They haven't said much about it.'

'Those two,' Mrs Denby sighed, 'are growing up cautious.'

'What do you mean?'

'Well, they don't accept things at face value any more. Too much has happened in their young lives. And I think even Delvene realises the days have gone when she can just arrive and dazzle them. But I have to admit she was honest about it.'

'She confided in you?'

'Yes, well, she said—thank God for Serena, she made me see I was living in cloud cuckoo land. They're not babies any more.'

There was silence for a minute or so, then Lorraine said, 'She always was . . . honest, wasn't she?'

'There are some things I can't ever forgive her for, honest or not.'

'Me neither. But to get back to Sean—would he just do it?' Lorraine's tone was wondering.

'Oh, he would—why shouldn't he?'

'Sean *can* be hard, I know, we all know, I guess.'

'If you ask me it's overdue—whether it's fair to Serena is another matter. Well,' said Denny, 'it's time I started doing something about dinner.'

Serena removed herself hastily, but for all the rest of that day she was puzzled. How *would* I react if I knew whatever it is I don't know? she asked herself. They obviously don't know Sean was honest with me.

Dinner was a Denny special, roast beef and Yorkshire

pudding, followed by a peach pie and cream, and Sean opened a bottle of wine. It was Des and Lorraine's last night.

To Richard and Cameron's delight, they were allowed to have a small glass of wine too.

'Sip it,' Sean advised.

'This is not the first time we've had wine,' Richard said importantly.

'Oh?'

'Mum took us out to dinner, didn't she, Denny?'

'Er . . . yes. If I remember correctly, you didn't like it,' Mrs Denby remarked.

'We didn't,' Cameron, who was incurably honest, said with a giggle.

'That was champagne,' Richard observed grandly. 'It was all fizzy, but,' despite himself his face wrinkled up in memory, 'pretty sour. This seems to be much nicer.' He held his glass up towards Sean.

'I'm so glad you approve,' Sean murmured straight-faced, but his eye caught Serena's and she had to turn away and pretend to have a cough.

The phone rang just as they had finished their peach pie and Mrs Denby, who was up collecting plates, went to answer it.

'For you, Sean,' she said, returning.

He cocked an eyebrow at her and a look of peculiar discomfort crossed her face. 'STD, by the sound of it.'

Sean's eyes narrowed, then he got up and went to take it in the study, closing the door firmly.

Serena thought nothing of it as she and Lorraine helped with the dishes. Sean often had long business phone calls. But it wasn't until much later, when she had changed into her nightgown and was sitting on their bed brushing her hair, that she saw him again.

Their master bedroom, by contrast to Des and Lorraine's, was old-fashioned but comfortable. There was a fireplace and a fire burning in the grate and casting flickering shadows on the ivory walls. Two comfortable basket chairs flanked the fireplace and were upholstered in an ivory and pink, small-figured chintz that matched the bedspread. It was a spacious room, and at first Rupert had been rather intimidated by the wide open spaces of the beautiful Persian carpet that stretched from the foot of the bed to the doors leading on to the veranda. But, only a couple of days later, he gambolled on it with the fluffy pompom Serena had made him as if it was his own private playing field, causing even Sean to observe that for a still very small and nondescript cat, he certainly knew how to enjoy himself, but did she think he realised the carpet was worth a small fortune?

She had grinned and replied that she was teaching him to have the utmost respect not only for the Persian carpet but all furniture and fittings.

But now, as she sat on the bed and brushed her hair, Rupert was curled up in his basket sound asleep, as was the rest of the household—at least, it was very quiet. Lorraine had gone to bed early, saying that the last couple of weeks of fresh country air and the twins' company had finally caught up with her. Mrs Denby had also retired early and Des had finally gone to join Sean in the study.

Even Des had gone to bed half an hour earlier, though, and Serena laid her brush down and was just about to go and see what was keeping Sean, when their bedroom door opened and he came in.

'I was just coming to get you,' she said with a smile, then it changed to a frown. 'Is something wrong?'

He didn't answer immediately but leant back against the closed door and folded his arms across his chest, his gaze resting on her impassively.

He had changed for dinner into his grey pincord jeans and grey shirt with a charcoal sweater, and his tawny hair was ruffled as if he had pulled a hand through it impatiently, perhaps several times. And perhaps because of his clothes, which reminded her of an interview she had once had with him in his study, or his expression or both, she heard herself saying uncertainly, 'Have I done something wrong?'

'Why should you imagine that?' he asked abruptly.

'I . . . I don't know,' she stammered. 'You look . . .' She stopped and gestured helplessly.

Sean straightened and came over to the bed, standing right in front of her with his hands shoved into his pockets and so that she had to tilt her head back to look up at him. She clasped her hands in her lap and pressed her knees nervously together.

He observed both small gestures and said barely audibly and with a nerve flickering in his jaw, 'Do you know how old you look at the moment?'

Serena glanced down at her fine pink Viyella nightgown that reached her ankles, at her bare feet, at her wrists enclosed in lace-trimmed Viyella as was her throat, and in a suddenly defensive movement, raised her hands to sweep her hair, which was loose and lying on her shoulders, up.

But Sean arrested the movement with a hand on her wrist. 'Don't—it doesn't help. It only makes you look as if you're playing at being older.'

Her lips parted and her eyes widened, and she flinched visibly and said his name on a breath.

'What?'

'Why . . . something's gone wrong, hasn't it?' she whispered. 'You . . . you've changed your mind about . . . about us.'

He stared down into her wide anguished eyes, his expression harsh, even a little mocking, she thought, and her breath rose in a small sob and she tried to wrest her wrist free.

Somehow, she wasn't sure how, she ended up lying back on the bed with Sean sitting beside her, her wrist still in his grasp. 'I haven't changed my mind,' he said very quietly, bending over her. 'I doubt if I ever will.' He released her wrist.

'Then why . . . Sean,' Serena said agitatedly as he started to unbutton her nightgown, 'please tell me, talk to me. I . . . I don't understand!'

'You wouldn't understand even if I told you,' he murmuredd, parting the pink Viyella and exposing her breasts. 'I barely understood myself. But since it's done . . .' He stopped and then with an impatient sound, gathered her up into his arms. 'Don't look like that.' And he started to kiss her.

Later, when the fire had all but burned down, Serena moved carefully and sat up to reach for her nightgown. Sean didn't stir.

She lay back, wide-eyed and a little shellshocked. Because his lovemaking had been intense, even bruising, and it was the first time it had been that way.

Something happened this evening, she thought,

staring at the ceiling. Something made him change—what could it have been? I must have done something . . .

But although she lay there and racked her brains, she could come up with nothing. In fact, she thought, he was perfectly fine until that telephone call, and I didn't even see him afterwards until . . .

She tensed suddenly. The phone call . . . Had it been about her? Ralph, perhaps, or her stepmother? Had Sean advised them of the marriage? But what on earth could they have come up with to make him so . . . the way he was?

She sighed forlornly, longing to seek the comfort and protection of his arms, but there was some sort of barrier between them now, she knew. She lay awake long into the early hours of the morning, then fell into a deep sleep.

Richard and Cameron woke her with the news that Des and Lorraine were due to leave shortly.

Serena dressed hurriedly when she realised she had slept through breakfast, wondering why no one had woken her earlier. There was no sign of Sean.

Mrs Denby was the first person she met. 'Why didn't you wake me up, Denny?'

'Sean said to let you sleep in, Serena. Here, I'll make you a cuppa—that's all you've got time for if you want to wave Des and Lorraine off.'

'Of course I want to! What must they think of me?'

'Because you slept in—only that you're still a new bride,' said Des over her shoulder.

She jumped and turned, to see that Sean was with him. 'Oh,' she coloured. 'I mean—oh!'

'We understand,' Lorraine whispered in her ear. 'Don't let them tease you.'

But although Sean smiled it was only a perfunctory one, and his eyes were curiously watchful. For the first time, Serena found herself unable to meet them.

But, by a conscious effort of will, she was able to project a cheerful image throughout the trip down to the airstrip and a genuinely grateful one to Des and Lorraine as they left.

Then, when the plane was no longer visible and the twins had stopped waving enthusiastically, Sean started to say something, but a stockman rode up to them, waving *his* hat furiously.

Sean swore beneath his breath, but as it transpired, another stockman had fallen off his horse while they had been moving a mob of cattle and been trampled. One of his legs was badly injured.

Having received this flood of information from the weary, breathless man on his horse beside the Land Rover, Sean didn't even waste time looking guilty. He gave the man some rapid instructions, then said briefly to the Land Rover party, 'I'll drop you back home.'

'Can't we come and see?' Richard enquired immediately.

'No, you cannot,' Sean said curtly. 'Denny, can you radio the Flying Doctor? Sounds as if we're going to need him—pity we just missed Bill.'

'All right,' Mrs Denby said calmly. 'Will you arrange for someone to meet him and drive him down?'

'Yes. Right, out you get.' Sean pulled the Land Rover up at the garden gate and the twins, looking disgruntled, hopped out with Mrs Denby. Sean put a hand on Serena's arm as she was about to alight, and she twisted to look at him.

'All right?' he said quietly.

'Fine,' she lied, lowering her lashes over her violet eyes so he wouldn't see the truth.

'I'll be back as soon as I can. Serena . . .'

'Of course. I hope he's all right—I'll keep my fingers crossed.' And she slipped out. For a moment, though, before she closed the door, she thought he was going to say something else, but in the end he didn't. And he drove off fast.

It was a long day. And the news they finally got was that Sean had accompanied the man in the air ambulance to its base hospital and would stay with him overnight.

'They're doing all they can to save his leg,' Bill, who had returned from delivering Des and Lorraine home, told them. 'But it's touch and go. Poor bloke—and he's only a kid really.'

Serena winced and for once was less than patient with Richard as she was putting the twins to bed, when he started to theorise on the difficulty of losing a leg.

'Just pray it won't happen,' she said shortly.

Richard looked briefly hurt. 'I only wondered . . .'

She sighed and ruffled his hair. 'I know. Look, I'll read you another story. That should send you to sleep.'

It did. But it left Serena to her own devices, which was something she'd been trying to avoid all day. Mrs Denby, who rose with the birds, had gone to bed too, and that only left Bill, another early bird who, although he didn't retire as early as Mrs Denby, liked to spend the last hour of his day reading in the quiet and privacy of his bedroom.

Serena changed and decided to go to bed herself, then changed her mind and wandered disconsolately into the study.

She sat down behind Sean's desk, fiddling with the sash of her blue candlewick dressing gown—and nearly jumped out of her skin when the phone rang.

Then with a fast-beating heart in case it was Sean, she answered it.

'Hello?'

There was some static and a series of clicks and pips, and she said hello again.

'Serena, is that you? I . . . er . . . it's Delvene.'

'Oh! Hello! How are you?'

There was a hesitation, then Delvene said quietly, 'Fine. Serena, is Sean there?'

Serena explained and asked, 'Can I take a message?'

'No,' said Delvene in that same uncharacteristically quiet way. 'By the way, congratulations,' she added.

Serena coloured and said a little breathlessly, 'Thank you—I wasn't sure if you knew. I . . . it happened rather unexpectedly.'

'Yes,' Delvene said down the line. 'As a matter of fact I didn't know until I rang Sean last night. Well . . .'

'You rang Sean last night?' Serena said blankly.

'Yes.' Delvene sounded strained and inexpressibly weary. 'Look, Serena, I won't keep you. Love to the twins! 'Bye now.'

Serena took the phone from her ear and stared at it. Then she closed her eyes, because she knew there had only been one phone call last night—and at last it all fell into place.

'Who was that?'

She jumped and looked up to see Bill standing in the doorway.

'Sean? Any news?' he queried, strolling into the room. 'Can't get the poor kid out of my mind,' he added.

'No. No, it was Delvene, Bill,' Serena said huskily, and replaced the receiver, 'Bill, were they in love once? Sean and Delvene, I mean?'

Bill's kindly, concerned expression changed slowly and a spark of anger lit his very blue eyes. 'What's she been telling you, Serena?'

CHAPTER NINE

'NOTHING!' Serena said hastily. 'Nothing.' She rubbed her brow distractedly. 'I've just . . . put it all together, that's all.'

'Young 'un you listen to me,' commanded Bill. 'It was all a long time ago—water under the bridge, that kind of thing.'

'Well . . .'

'And don't let her tell you any different—matter of fact, she's caused enough ruckus in this family, but it's *you* Sean married, whatever happened years ago.'

Serena was very pale, but she said steadily enough, 'Did she hope Sean would marry her?'

'If she did, she misread him,' Bill said grimly. 'He's not the type to lust after his brother's wife.'

'So they didn't meet, Sean and Delvene, until *after* she'd married Andrew?'

'No . . . listen, there's one person to tell you about it and that's Sean himself, Serena.'

'Oh, he did.'

'Then why are you looking like this?' Bill demanded.

'He . . . he didn't tell me who . . . it was.'

Bill was silent for a moment. Then he said, 'Does that make a difference?'

It does . . . I don't know why, but it *does*,' Serena

whispered to Rupert, who was curled up in her lap as she sat in a basket chair before the fire in the bedroom. Somehow or other she had managed to reassure Bill that it had just come as a bit of a shock but that she would be fine. And, ostensibly, she had come to bed.

But sleep was the furthest thing from her mind now. 'Why didn't he tell me?' she mused. 'I . . . oh! That's what Denny and Lorraine were talking about—not how I would react but how Delvene would react to the news of our marriage. I think . . . I think she must have reacted badly enough to really upset Sean . . . he was so strange last night, as if it was something he shouldn't have done . . . marrying me.'

She closed her eyes and laid her head back with a sigh, wondering how she could have been so blind in the first place. Then her mind reverted to the question that puzzled her most—Sean had been honest with her up to a point. He had told her about a love that had gone wrong . . . why hadn't he told her it was Delvene? She was bound to find out sooner or later.

'Because I wouldn't have married him if I'd known? I wouldn't have, either,' she whispered. 'It's one thing to know about some faceless woman he couldn't have, although that's not quite the way it is, but it's altogether another thing to actually *know* her and even like her . . . to have to wonder if Sean married me to . . . sort of punish her. She even said that, didn't she? When are you going to stop punishing me?'

A slient tear slid down her cheek and she licked it off her lip as the next question formed itself in her mind. What is it that keeps them apart like this? she asked herself. I could understand it if she was still married to his brother, even if Andrew was still alive, but now . . .

Did—despite the fact that he fell in love with her—did Sean hate her for coming between him and his brother . . . and then Andrew *died* so it was even worse? And then she's so independent, isn't she? She may want him and love him desperately, but she'd still want to keep her career, I think. Not like me who, in every respect but one, is the perfect wife for Sean Wentworth. But that one respect is that he happens to love another woman . . . I don't know how I can live with that. Not in these circumstances . . . I think I might have to leave before it all gets incredibly tangled and we all hurt each other even more . . .

She stood up and put Rupert gently back in his basket, then suddenly she whirled around and ran to the bed and flung herself down on it, face down.

'I loved him so much,' she wept. 'How could he do this to me? But I'm going to show him . . . what?'

She twisted round and sat up with her face in her hands. 'That you can't stand the hurt?' she muttered. 'Yes!' she answered herself. 'Also that he thinks I'm child enough not to *understand* . . . I understand very well now, and I'm leaving, but I'm also going to write you a note, Sean Wentworth, and in that note I'm going to tell you a few facts of life. It's all very well being hard and unforgiving, but the only way you're going to be happy is if you *do* forgive her. Is it such a crime to find out you married the wrong man? How long has she got to pay for that? The rest of her life?'

'. . . And that's why I'm leaving, Sean. Don't worry about me,' Serena wrote. 'At least one good thing has come out of it, I'm free and independent now. Would you mind very much looking after Rupert for me?'

She stopped and bit the end of the pen, then wrote again. 'In spite of the way things have turned out, I'll always be grateful to you for saving me from Ralph. Serena.'

She read and re-read the note, then folded it carefully and impatiently dashed away her tears. 'All I've got to do now is figure out how to get off the place. I'm quite sure Bill wouldn't fly me . . . I wonder, I know I've never done it before—well, apart from the odd lesson before Dad died, but I've seen it done so often . . . yes, that's it.'

'That's a good Land Rover,' Serena said several hours later, just before the dawn broke, 'you started like a charm. Now all we've got to do is follow the track to the short boundary, which is only about fifty miles, I know, and there it meets the main Goondiwindi road. I can thumb a lift from there . . . oh, God, don't look back, Serena. What will Denny think, and the twins? She'll probably be worried sick, but with Bill already out and Sean away there won't be much she can do, and by the time there is, let's hope I'll be far away enough for them not to be able to track me down. Just . . . go.'

Three hours later, when the fifty-mile trip to the boundary should only have taken her an hour or perhaps a little longer, Serena acknowledged that she was lost, she was frightened and the Land Rover had mysteriously died on her.

'Perhaps I mangled the gears so much,' she whispered, 'it's taking its revenge, but it just won't go—what am I going to do?'

She stared around distractedly. She had been on some sort of a track all the time, but for the last half hour it had wandered apparently aimlessly through stands of mulga and rough tussocky grass, then it had simply petered out. That was when she had decided to stop and consider her position—and when she had foolishly turned the engine off.

But when her considerations had indicated that the only thing to do was to turn around and retrace her way to where she must have unwittingly turned off the right track, the Land Rover had refused to start.

'I'll have to walk,' she said out loud, then shivered as she remembered the last time she had made a decision like that, and the consequences. 'But I do have a track to follow this time,' she added to herself, 'and it's not dark, I can have a good drink of water out of the water bag on the front—I can take it with me! I have everything going for me,' she finished with more confidence.

Then she looked around again at the wide, winter-blue sky, at the endless landscape apparently uninhabited by so much as a solitary sheep, and was overcome for a moment by a feeling of sheer insignificance and helplessness. 'Why don't I stop to think before I do these things?' she whispered. 'Perhaps I'm still more of a child than I realise.'

It was at that painful moment that the dashboard buzzed, definitely buzzed.

Serena stared at it and the instruments, her heart started to pound and she thought, of course, that's got to be a two-way radio or a CB or something, that's why there's such a long aerial—why didn't I think . . . of that?

Her hand hovered and her mouth went dry, because she knew, just knew it would be Sean, perhaps more angry than he'd ever been with her—but not to answer it? Wouldn't that be compounding her foolishness?

She picked up the receiver and pressed a button.

'H-hello?'

'Serena?' It was Sean's voice, and even the static couldn't disguise the harsh coldness of his tone. 'Is that you?'

She licked her lips. 'Yes. Yes, it's me, Sean.'

There was a pause and she thought she heard a sigh but knew it was only her imagination when he demanded, 'Where the bloody hell are you?'

'I . . . don't know . . .'

'You don't know—I might have guessed,' he said sardonically. 'At least you're still with the Land Rover, though, small mercy, but I didn't know you drove.'

Serena swallowed. 'I don't actually have a licence, but I have had a couple of lessons and I got this far with no trouble, only . . . now I'm stuck. It . . . it won't start.'

'You seem to imagine Land Rovers are machines capable of magic,' he said with irony. 'If you've been driving all this time, you've probably run out of petrol,' he added drily.

Serena bit her lip.

'All right,' he said abruptly, 'I want you to try and describe the track you took—I presume you did take one—and *then* I want you to stay put. Do you understand me, Serena?'

'I . . . yes.'

*   *   *

He came, not in another Land Rover as she had expected but on his horse, and leading Sally.

Serena was sitting dejectedly on the bonnet and she didn't hear him until she looked up and twisted round at the sound of a twig cracking, and he was there, tall and forbidding astride his black horse, dressed all in khaki and with a wide-brimmed hat on.

'Oh!' she exclaimed, and put a hand to her mouth. 'You gave me a fright!'

Sean regarded her steadily for a moment, then dismounted and tied the horses to a tree. 'You gave a lot of people a fright, Serena,' he said quietly, coming up to the bonnet of the Land Rover.

She found she couldn't look into those grey-green eyes and with a muffled sob, she buried her face in her hands, thereby considerably adding to the dirty streaks on it.

'Nor are tears going to help,' he added, taking her wrists and pulling her hands from her face. 'Look at me,' he commanded softly.

When she did it was with an inner shrinking, because she knew he must be very angry with her, and her drenched violet eyes were scared but also stubborn. 'I'm sorry . . . about that,' she whispered, 'but you shouldn't have done what you did, Sean.'

He released her wrists and took her chin in his hand. 'I take it you're referring to the subject of that long letter you left for me—how to rectify the state of my life in two easy steps, in other words, courtesy of a little girl who considers herself a veritable fount of wisdom on the subject . . .'

'I'm not a little girl,' Serena broke in mutinously.

'You certainly act like one sometimes,' he commented, and traced a tear stain down her cheek, 'but you agreed to this marriage and . . .'

'Because I didn't *know*,' Serena said desperately. 'I didn't know it was Delvene. I tried to explain in the letter that . . . why . . .' She stopped and blinked. 'I don't want to talk about it any more,' she said then with as much dignity as she could muster. 'I'm sorry if you don't understand how I feel, but I can't change it, and that's why I'm going to go, Sean, somehow.' And her violet eyes were suddenly challenging.

'You're very haughty,' he said softly after a moment, with an enigmatic glint in his eye.

She caught her breath but looked away, and her expression was proud despite the dirty marks on her cheeks and her general state of dishevelment—her hair had come tumbling down from the knot she had tied it up in, and three hours of wrestling the Land Rover over a bush track had left her jeans and blouse sweaty and crumpled.

'Also angry with me, I think,' Sean observed into the silence.

Serena looked down at her hands and then around at the hot, still bush, the patient horses standing with their muzzles touching and their tails lazily switching the flies away.

'Yes, I am,' she said, and went on intensely, 'You *should* have told me. But you persist in treating me like a child, even a retarded child, and now . . .' her voice faltered, 'look where I am!'

'Up the creek without a paddle, as that old saying goes?' he suggested.

Her violet eyes blazed and for a moment she felt like hitting him. 'No!' she said through her teeth. 'You'll see—I'll manage.'

'Serena,' he said in a different voice, 'I had thought that you were . . . you weren't unhappy about being married to me.'

She lowered her lashes. 'I wasn't,' she answered tautly. 'And if you must know, I even think I'd be a much better wife for you!'

'So . . .' he said slowly.

'But it doesn't work that way,' she cried, looking up. 'Not when you love her and she loves you and . . . and . . . Sean,' her voice changed as he put his hands around her waist, 'what are you doing!'

'Lifting you down,' he drawled, suiting action to words but keeping his hands on her waist when she was on her feet.

'Sean . . .'

'And I'm going to make you a cup of billy tea, over which we can sort this out once and for all. Have you a set of really warm clothes in your bag?'

'I . . . yes,' she stammered, 'but I don't understand—I'm *hot!*'

'You won't be tonight.'

'Tonight—Sean,' she licked her lips, 'what are you going to do with me?'

A fleeting smile touched his lips. 'Don't look so frightened. We're going to camp out tonight.'

'*Why?*'

'Why, Mrs Wentworth?' he said idly. 'Because in view of your propensity for fleeing into the bush and getting lost, I think it's time I gave you some bushcraft lessons. Then,' he raised a hand and brushed some strands of hair out of her eyes, 'if you're still possessed of a burning desire to run away from me, you might be more successful about it—that's why.'

Serena sipped her tea in a frustrated sort of silence. She couldn't help feeling she'd missed something somewhere along the line, because as he had made the fire and boiled the billy, spread out a groundsheet in the shade and given the horses a drink, Sean had been different—apparently not even angry any more.

'Sean,' Serena said tentatively as he came back from the horses and stretched out on the groundsheet opposite her, propped up on one elbow.

He pulled his hat off and ran a hand through his hair. 'Yes?'

But she couldn't put her thoughts into words.

He waited for a time, absently fiddling with the handle of his mug. Then he looked up and straight into her eyes and said softly, 'Serena, if I once imagined myself in love with Delvene, it's no longer the case. It hasn't been really since I rescued a . . . violet-eyed waif from a gutter.'

Serena's mouth trembled and she tried to speak, but again no words would come.

'What you told me in your letter,' he went on, 'your understanding,' he added drily, 'of how it all happened in the first place was pretty accurate. I'd been overseas studying stock breeding and management for nearly a year and while I was away, Andy married Delvene. By the time I got home, although she was pregnant, it was pretty obvious things weren't going to work out for them. It was also pretty obvious,' he said wearily, 'that some sort of magnetism seemed to flow between *us,* although, God help me, I *never* understood how I could want a woman

I . . . despised.'

He looked down at his mug again and Serena stared at the harsh lines of his face with her lips parted.

'But however much I tried to deny it, to stamp it out, to . . . ignore her, Andy sensed it. He knew, and he knew not only what she was unable to hide but what I was trying to conceal. So he took her away to Sydney, because that was the other thing she wanted. Six months later, Richard and Cameron were born. Two years later, Andy came back to Rosewood with them and told me he and Delvene were getting divorced. He was . . . he was devastated, and to this day, I don't know if it was his state of mind that led to the accident.'

Serena gasped.

'Oh, he didn't commit suicide, but he was withdrawn, inattentive and . . . well, a lapse of concentration would have done it. If you could imagine how I felt . . .'

'Yes! But . . . but you'd done nothing—I mean,' Serena explained, 'you can't help how you react to people, can you, but you hadn't . . .'

'No, we hadn't,' Sean said flatly.

'And she wasn't the right wife for him anyway,' Serena said into the silence.

'Be that as it may, she *was* his wife.'

'So,' Serena said barely audibly, 'you've . . . for the last six years you've held her responsible for it all. Did you . . . even marry me to punish her more?'

Sean sat up and leant back against the trunk of the tree shading them. 'I decided to marry you . . . in the heat of the moment,' he said.

Serena flinched beneath his grey-green gaze.

'And with not the least thought of Delvene on my mind,' he added. 'I married you because I couldn't bear the thought of you being hurt or frightened, because I couldn't tolerate the idea of anyone else making love to you.' He smiled slightly. 'Because I never could walk away from you, not even after that first night when I thought you might be . . . heaven knows what.'

'But you did,' she whispered.

'Did I? I also went around to the Pelican Club the next day,' he admitted. 'It was the fourth such establishment I visited trying to track you down, with some idea of wresting you from it. That's how I knew you'd been sacked.'

The wheels of Serena's mind spun furiously. 'I *meant* to ask you how you knew that!'

'And if you hadn't pipped me to the post by applying for the job, I knew where you lived and fully intended to visit you to see if you'd decided to take my advice.'

Serena stared at him wide-eyed.

'All of which goes to prove,' he said with a strange little smile twisting his lips, 'that from the moment I met you it would be fair to say that you intrigued me and fascinated me. To be honest, also exasperated me, and a few other things, but the fascination was there all along. What got in its way,' Sean went on deliberately as she tried to speak, 'was . . . well, a couple of things. I'm sorry if I've treated you like a child from time to time, but you *are* very young and, it became increasingly obvious, very innocent. Then,' he paused, 'there was myself. I kept thinking—this can't be happening to me.'

'Sean . . . why not?' she whispered.

He shrugged wearily and looked straight into her eyes. 'When you've lived on a treadmill of desire and hate, attraction and disgust, self-disgust, for as long as I had, when you've deliberately taken out a succession of women to make yourself forget or in the hope that this one or that one will be the one to erase it all and it hasn't, it's very hard to believe when it does happen. But when it's someone you know you *shouldn't* . . . even consider . . .'

A tear fell on to Serena's hand as she said, 'Not ever? I mean . . .'

'Oh, I had planned to wait, Serena,' Sean said softly. 'I thought, after Ralph—well, at least I've got some time on my side now. Time for her to grow up and sort out whether it's me she loves or the fact that I saved her from an ugly, frightening situation. Time for her to get over her fear of men . . . But the very next day, I knew I couldn't wait any longer and I . . . gave you no choice about it,' he said sombrely.

'Well . . . well,' she said haltingly, 'although I didn't know what to do then, after I'd done it . . . it was fine with me,' she said tremulously. 'But . . .'

'But if I'd told you about Delvene, *would* you have understood?' he queried. 'Or would you have felt conscience-stricken, as you did last night?'

Serena twisted her hands. 'But I had to find out some time, Sean. And when I realised . . . I mean, I worked out that you'd changed after that phone call, and when I knew it was her, all the little bits and pieces fell into place. The way you were . . .'

Sean closed his eyes briefly. 'Come here,' he said very quietly.

Serena hesitated, then crept into his arms.

'Did I hurt you?' he queried.

'No . . . but you made me feel . . . I thought, one call from her and you were already regretting us.'

'Which is precisely why I didn't know how to tell you it was her. Can you understand that? And I reasoned, again in the heat of the moment, that by the time you did find out, it would be too late.'

'Then . . . what happened?' Serena asked shakily.

Sean smoothed her hair and gathered her closer. 'When I told her about us, she accused me of marrying a starstruck little girl with an adolescent crush on me to . . . because I couldn't forgive her for Andy. And I knew she was partly right. 'Not,' he stopped as Serena flinched, and he slid his fingers through hers, 'not the second bit, but I *had* . . . manipulated you into marrying me. I hadn't even told you the truth,' he added drily, 'and not only about her. I was very cautious—even cunning—because although I knew you looked upon me as some sort of knight in shining armour, I was afraid a passionate declaration of love might frighten you, so I took it very slowly and gently. I also appealed to that rather soft heart of yours and, I think, made you feel you could repay the debt you felt you owed me by marrying me, seeing there was no hope for my . . . other love.'

'Oh . . . you did,' Serena confessed.

'Whereas what was really in *my* heart,' he said rather grimly, 'was the conviction that you were mine, whether you liked it or not, or were too young to know your own mind, and that no other man was going to be given the opportunity not only to hurt or frighten you, but to change that.'

'Sean . . .?' Serena stared up at him dazedly. 'Oh, I didn't know . . . do you really feel like that?'

His eyes softened. 'I'm afraid so. But I do, occasionally, also feel as guilty as hell about rushing you like that and . . . deceiving you. When Delvene said what she did it was one of those occasions.'

'Sean . . . oh, Sean!' she whispered, and reached up to touch his face. 'Do you know how I feel when I'm not with you? It's as if all the lights have gone out, it's not only frightening but it's lonelier than I've ever been. Do you know what it's like when I . . . when I see you with someone else?'

He frowned. 'When . . . who?'

'At the party—you were talking to a woman in a gold dress with dark hair and you were looking at her . . . sort of . . .'

Sean smiled slightly. 'My darling Serena,' he murmured, 'right up until I found Reg Findlay putting the hard word on you, I was doing my damnedest to stick to,' he grimaced, 'Plan A. Which involved not only will-power, a battle I lost, but some subterfuge. I can't even remember her name.'

'Oh. Well, I wish I'd known, because I felt . . . very miserable and jealous and all sorts of horrible things, and it's at times like those that I feel my world has fallen apart and I do . . . I do crazy things like this,' Serena said softly.

He cupped her cheek. 'My world goes mad. I fight people, and not only physically—you've no idea the mayhem I created this morning when I got home and found you gone and everyone running around in circles!'

Serena winced.

'I'll make it up to them,' he promised.

'They might even understand,' she said huskily. 'You see, they're all convinced I'm the best thing that ever happened to you and they never doubted that I adore you!'

'They've told you this?' he queried.

'They've told each other,' her lips trembled into a smile, 'I just happened to overhear.'

'Did you now?' His eyes glinted. 'All those people I was so unkind to this morning, I suppose?'

'Some of them.'

'Then you think it's right for us to . . . resume our marriage?' His gaze was intent until she nodded. 'In that case, I think you ought to kiss me now,' he recommended, tracing the outline of her mouth. 'It seems to tame the monster in me.'

She did.

'So all along this is what you planned to do with me tonight,' Serena said dreamily.

'Mmm . . . with or without your consent. I even had darker plans for you.'

She smiled a secret little smile. 'I can imagine.'

They were ensconced on the floor of the Land Rover with the light of the fire Sean had built up outside flickering on the rolled-down canvas sides—and it had been a day to remember despite its disastrous beginning. Sean had come well prepared with food and after radioing Bill that all was well, true to his word, he had not only shown her some more wonders of the bush but he had also given her some bushcraft lessons. Then as the swift, chilly night had drawn in, he had made the fire and cooked them dinner, and built it up to last for hours—then prepared their bed for the night.

'Can you?' he drawled, moving the blankets aside so he could view her totally naked body at his leisure. 'Cold?'

'No . . .' But she trembled at his touch.

'Tell me what you imagined,' he invited, playing with her nipples.

'Well,' she said softly, 'you once told *me* . . .'

Sean groaned and looked into her eyes ruefully.

'That if you had any sense,' Serena continued demurely, 'you'd put me over your knee and beat the living daylights out of me just to teach me to stop and think before I commit these rash acts . . .'

'If I'd known,' he broke in, 'that you were going to memorise every damn thing I said to you . . .'

'You'd have been much nicer to me and not threatened me with violence?' she teased.

'Perhaps,' he conceded, his eyes laughing at her. 'But you got it wrong.'

'I did?'

'Yes,' he said gravely. 'That might have been all right for naughty schoolgirls, but married ladies require different treatment.'

'They do?' Serena murmured innocently, raising her arm idly because he had returned his attention to her breasts, causing her to be invaded by a sensuous languor. She slid her fingers through his hair and down his neck. 'Treatment even darker than this?' she queried.

'Along the same lines, but, because of my black sense of doom this morning, I thought I'd keep doing it until I got you pregnant.'

'So I couldn't run away again?'

'Uh-huh . . . something like that.'

'I see.'

'Whereas in my more rational moments, I think that might be something we should postpone for a while. What do you think?'

'Because I'm too young?' Serena asked seriously.

'Because I want you to myself for a while,' Sean answered. Then he said, 'You may not have noticed what's happening to me . . .'

'I have,' she whispered.

'Well, in view of your conviction that you're the perfect wife for me . . .'

'I didn't say that!' But she snuggled into his arms, smiling tenderly.

'It was something very similar, I'm sure.'

'And it's about time I proved it. Is that it?'

'Yes. Love me?'

'More than ever . . . oh!'

'What now?'

'I forgot to ask you about the stockman.'

'He's going to be fine. Anything else?' He raised a quizzical eyebrow at her.

'No-o . . .'

'But?'

'Sean—what are we going to do about Delvene?' Serena's violet eyes were hesitant but serious.

He sighed. 'I wondered when you were going to start to worry about her again.'

'I couldn't help liking her, you see.'

'I know.' He caressed her throat and drew her head into his shoulder. 'What can I say? Now that the years of torment are ended for me, I can only be sorry that it hasn't yet ended for her. But perhaps this—us—will help. In fact, that's what she rang to tell me last night—the call you took.'

'Oh!' Serena moved to look up into his eyes.

'She rang again this morning,' he said. 'To apologise for the things she'd said and also to say that she intended to try to put it all behind her now and . . . to organise her life better so that Richard and Cameron can spend as much time as possible with her. I said that while we would always love them and treat them as our own, for their sakes and for *her* sake, she should do that. I don't mean,' he added as Serena tensed, 'suddenly uprooting them from Rosewood, but at least stepping up *your* plan to integrate them into her life. She said she'd suddenly realised how precious they were to her—and she felt very guilty that it had taken something like this to make her understand.'

Serena blinked away a tear and he kissed her eyelids. 'I think I persuaded her to believe I was as much to blame for that but that we should . . . put our guilt behind us and concentrate on what's best for them and her.'

Serena slid her arms around his neck.

'All right?' he asked.

'Yes,' she said softly. 'Just one last thing. Thank you for a lovely day.'

'Serena,' Sean's voice was curiously uneven and he tightened his embrace almost unbearably for a moment, then relaxed with a sigh, 'I adore you.'

Harlequin Presents®

Coming Next Month

1191 NO WAY TO SAY GOODBYE Kay Gregory
Gareth Mardon closes his Vancouver office and heartlessly dismisses the staff.
Roxane Peters is furious—and she has no compunctions about making her
feelings quite clear to Gareth. Only somehow, it seems, her feelings are
threatened, too....

1192 THE HEAT IS ON Sarah Holland
When Steve Kennedy erupts into Lorel's life, she has the very uncomfortable
feeling she's met him before. Yet it's impossible to ignore him, for he proves to
be the screenwriter on the film in which she wants the leading role.

1193 POTENTIAL DANGER Penny Jordan
Young Kate had been too passionately in love to care about the future. Now a
mature woman, Kate has learned to take care of herself and her daughter. But
no matter how she tries she can't stop loving Silas Edwards, the man who
betrayed her.

1194 DEAL WITH THE DEVIL Sandra Marton
Elena marries Blake Rogan to get out of her revolution-torn country on an
American passport. She believes Rogan married her in a deal with her father
for hard cash. But Rogan just wants to get out alive—with or without Elena.

1195 SWEET CAPTIVITY Kate Proctor
Kidnapped and imprisoned along with famous film director Pascal de
Perregaux, Jackie is prey to all sorts of feelings. Most disturbing is her
desperate attraction to Cal, her fellow victim—especially since he believes she
is in league with their abductors....

1196 CHASE THE DAWN Kate Walker
Desperate for money to restore her little sister's health, Laurel approaches her
identical twin sister's estranged husband. She's forgotten just how much like
her twin she looks—and she finds herself impersonating her sister and
"married" to the formidable Hal Rochester.

1197 DRIVING FORCE Sally Wentworth
Maddy's divorce from racing-car driver West Marriott was painful. He is no
longer part of her life. Now West needs her professional help after an accident.
Maddy isn't sure, though, that she can treat her ex-husband as just
another client!

1198 WHEN THE GODS CHOOSE Patricia Wilson
Arrogant Jaime Carreras is the most insulting man Sara has ever met. Why
should she care what he thinks of her? Unfortunately, however, Jaime is the
only man who can help her trace her father in the wilds of Mexico.

Available in August wherever paperback books are sold, or through
Harlequin Reader Service:

In the U.S.
901 Fuhrmann Blvd.
P.O. Box 1397
Buffalo, N.Y. 14240-1397

In Canada
P.O. Box 603
Fort Erie, Ontario
L2A 5X3

You'll flip . . . your pages won't!
Read paperbacks *hands-free* with

Book Mate • I

The perfect "mate" for all your romance paperbacks

**Traveling • Vacationing • At Work • In Bed • Studying
• Cooking • Eating**

Perfect size for all standard paperbacks, this wonderful invention makes reading a pure pleasure! Ingenious design holds paperback books OPEN and FLAT so even wind can't ruffle pages – leaves your hands free to do other things. Reinforced, wipe-clean vinyl-covered holder flexes to let you turn pages without undoing the strap . . . supports paperbacks so well, they have the strength of hardcovers!

Pages turn WITHOUT opening the strap.

SEE-THROUGH STRAP

Reinforced back stays flat

Built in bookmark

BOOK MARK

BACK COVER HOLDING STRIP

10" x 7¼" opened.
Snaps closed for easy carrying, too

Harlequin Regency Romance™

Romance the way it was *always* meant to be!

The time is 1811, when a Regent Prince rules the empire. The place is London, the glittering capital where rakish dukes and dazzling debutantes scheme and flirt in a dangerously exciting game. Where marriage is the passport to wealth and power, yet every girl hopes secretly for love....

Welcome to Harlequin Regency Romance where reading is an adventure and romance is *not* just a thing of the past! Two delightful books a month.

Available wherever Harlequin Books are sold.